DIAMOND
IN THE BUFF

SUSAN DUNLAP

A DELL BOOK

For Carlyle Gordon

Published by
Dell Publishing
a division of
Bantam Doubleday Dell Publishing Group, Inc.
666 Fifth Avenue
New York, New York 10103

ISBN: 0-440-20788-6

Reprinted by arrangement with St. Martin's Press

Printed in the United States of America

Published simultaneously in Canada

May 1991

10 9 8 7 6 5 4 3 2 1

OPM

Acknowledgments

A special thanks to Berkeley Police Lieutenant Stan Muller and the detectives in Homicide–Felony Assault Detail for their invaluable help in answering my questions.

i

THERE'S a saying in Buddhist lore I heard somewhere: The way to domesticate a horse is to put him in a fenced pasture, but make that pasture so big he never sees the fence. Thus both horse and owner are satisfied.

In Berkeley, California, we've got the biggest pasture around. We take pride in our openness. But the problem with an endless pasture is that it fences in some rather odd horses. And there's not one of us in it who wouldn't raise an eyebrow at half the other equines in the field.

The combination of a three-year drought and now a sudden heat wave had squeezed our fences as close as those on the ramp to the glue factory. Tolerance was getting rare as green grass. By the third day of the heat wave everyone was acting strange. At any other time, if Farley, the dispatcher, had called me to a 245 (felony assault) like the one he had today, I would have thought it was a joke. As it was, I did wonder if the heat was getting to Farley.

By this third steaming day, the few sleeveless tops any of us owned were in the hamper. We'd all spent two nights when it was too hot to eat, to hot to sleep, and, it

1

was a fair guess, too hot to touch the person lying next to us. Too hot, that is, for anyone who had not repressed her hunger for Seth Howard for two years, wary of the dangers of being involved with another detective on the force, for anyone who had not seen Howard's curly red hair shake as he laughed day after day, who had not sat virtually knee to knee in a tiny office, watching his big grin spread slowly, inexorably across his face, like a finger running up the inside of a thigh, till the grin burst into great guffaws and my whole body quivered. Talk about stress on the job!

But no one said being a homicide detective was easy.

Even up here, high in the hills in The Palace, where I was housesitting, everything was almost too hot to touch. But there were four showers in The Palace bathrooms, one with five spigots, and all big enough for an orgy. Howard and I had managed to deal with touch remarkably well, an accomplishment that had made the nights considerably better than the mornings that followed.

Now at noon, Howard was in one of the showers and I was still under the all-cotton sheet in the California King–size bed (the domestic equivalent of the endless pasture).

But I had to be out of here (out of both the California King and The Palace around it) by the weekend. Apartment hunting was my reason for taking the day off. Helping to apartment hunt was Howard's.

I picked up the East Bay *Express* and turned to the ads. But after living in this house with its wine cellar, hot tub, sauna, three decks, and a nightly view of the sun setting behind San Francisco, moving to even the best apartment in town was like replacing an elegant Arabian stallion with a mule.

Howard stuck his head out of the bathroom. He was wearing a blue towel I'd gotten him from the L.L. Bean catalog and he had one arm in a T-shirt from the slide

2

show/lecture on a Himalayan climbing expedition we'd been to last night. He shoved the other arm in and pulled the shirt over his head. It was too short, not an uncommon occurrence for someone six-six.

I laughed.

"Thanks a lot," Howard grumbled. "Another of my shirts you inherit."

"It's kind of apt, don't you think?" I said, reaching over to run a finger beneath the hem. "It ends abruptly, like the lecture itself."

Howard flopped on the bed. "I'll tell you, Jill, Bev Zagoya's lucky she's a mountaineer and not a full-time lecturer. She's got no sense of timing. She spends an hour on the tedious preliminaries to the climb, and then she spots a blond guy in the back of the room, decides she's got better ways to spend her evening, and rips through the tale of the climb to the summit like the cops are after her." He grinned and wriggled closer till his leg brushed mine through the sheet. "A condition you might consider yourself."

"Okay, Detective." I started to toss the newspaper aside, but Howard caught my arm and laughed.

"Finally got to the ads, huh?"

I groaned.

"Well, Jill, my offer stands. I've got the best house in Berkeley—"

"*This* is the best house in Berkeley."

For no more than an instant the skin around Howard's eyes tightened and his jaw dropped. In less than a second he was laughing. But I knew the sore spot I'd poked. His house was no mule. But it wasn't an Arabian either. Except to him. To Howard the shabby six-bedroom brown shingle in which he was chief renter, of which he yearned to be owner, was Kentucky Derby material.

3

That wasn't making my days of apartment hunting any easier. It wasn't making my nights better, either.

The phone rang. I picked it up with relief. Momentary relief. It was the call from the dispatcher. Calling on my day off. Right then I knew it was not a good sign.

"Smith?"

"Right, Farley."

"You've got a two forty-five on Panoramic Way. Pereira did the prelim."

Assault with a deadly weapon. In Homicide–Felony Assault we get plenty of assaults. We don't get called in on days off to do the follow-up. Definitely not a good sign. "Did Pereira say what the deadly weapon was?"

Farley paused. I could have sworn I heard a laugh. What kind of sign was that? "Yeah."

"And our victim was assaulted with . . . ?" I prompted.

"A eucalyptus."

ASSAULT by eucalyptus! Even in the giant pasture of Berkeley, that was a new one. The guilty party, according to the dispatcher, was one *Eucalyptus camaldulensis*. It was going to be a helluva report to write.

I did a quick brush of makeup, grabbed a denim jacket (R.E.I. catalog), and was headed for the front door when the phone rang again. I hesitated before picking up the cordless phone next to the bed. I hated to leave Pereira standing in the scorching sun next to a 120-foot-tall "responsible."

"Smith? It's Murakawa." Paul Murakawa was a patrol officer. His calling me at home in the middle of the day was not-good sign number two.

"I'm on my way to a two forty-five," I said, walking into the hall. "What's up?"

"Oh. Well, I got this call. The complainant's in my district. I wouldn't contact you officially . . ."

I stepped into the living room. The front door was thirty feet away. I'd leave the phone there. "Then why don't I call you—"

". . . but I thought you should handle it," he said in

one burst of breath. If I'd had any question about not-good, Murakawa's insistence answered it. Murakawa was young, athletic, and had more energy and drive than any other horse in the pasture. I had never heard Murakawa asking anyone to do work for him. Not until now. Not-good, indeed.

I stopped. "Okay. What?"

"Mr. Kepple."

My former landlord. Triple Crown quality not-good.

"The neighbors," he said.

"Again."

"They didn't file a complaint, *this* time. But someone needs to talk to Mr. Kepple." I could almost see Murakawa shaking his head. And I could almost see a smile, so slight that it would alert only the most perceptive soul to Paul Murakawa's relief that it was not he who was going to deal with Mr. Kepple. But I could appreciate that smile; if I could have passed the buck to someone else I would have been grinning ear to ear.

"I'll go by after the two forty-five," I said.

"The two forty-five? That the call on Panoramic Way?"

"Right. The assault by eucalyptus."

Murakawa hung up. He was laughing.

I plunked the phone back in its holder and headed for my car. As I drove down the hill I thought about Mr. Kepple and his electric mower, blower, and hedge clipper, Mr. Kepple and his earphones. I wondered when was the last time Mr. Kepple had *listened* to anyone, and I contemplated my impending afternoon with a malicious eucalyptus and an oblivious ex-landlord. Murakawa's example of professional courtesy was exactly the reason cops had no private lives.

At the station I changed cars. In a city that is self-insured, it doesn't pay to take your own car anywhere on duty. In an accident, collecting from *your* insurance company would suit the city fine.

The patrol car was hot as a hibachi. I drove east across Telegraph Avenue. The sidewalks were crowded with street artists and shorts-clad University of California students licking ice cream cones. The scene reminded me that I hadn't had time for the ice cream I'd envisioned for breakfast. This is the reason cops don't have decent food lives. I drove on past the fraternity houses and the Cal Bears football stadium.

Half a block later the road ended at the bottom of the sharp surge of hills.

Panoramic Way begins there. Looking at the abrupt rise of the hills, it is easy to imagine one tectonic plate sliding under another, crumpling its edge and creating the Berkeley Hills and the Hayward fault.

And yet the feel of Panoramic Way is not the wild temporariness of buildings hanging off the edge of an earthquake fault. It's more like an old, hillside English village with vine-covered, leaded-windowed cottages that squat up against the sidewalk. The street veers back and forth up the hillside. The pavement is so narrow that when cars meet, the descending one must back up till there is a spot to pull over and the uphill driver can squeeze by. At the first three corners the road cuts back sharply like the sides of a clown's mouth. To make the turn, a driver has to get right to the outside edge of pavement and cut the wheel so hard the tires squeal.

Across from my call site a retaining wall held up the ground. Redwoods and live oaks grew above it and vines dangled over the edge. And under them Mazdas and ancient Porsches were wedged against the wall by the NO PARKING ANY TIME signs. (That's how hidden our fences are!)

Patrol Officer Connie Pereira was standing on the curb. Pereira was my closest friend in the department. We'd been to conferences, parties, all-night stakeouts; at

7

dawn, Connie Pereira always looked as good as she did at dusk. I'd never seen her show the effects of a wait.

Until now. Pereira must have been waiting here about half an hour. She looked like it'd been half a century. Any curl in her blond hair was gone; it hung limp over her damp forehead. Her eye makeup was gone, leaving pale blue lines down her cheeks. Her skin was not tan but the color of soggy squash. And with all that, she was smiling.

I pulled the patrol car in front of the driveway. It was the only empty spot, legal or otherwise. Pereira hurried over. Closer up I could see the stains of perspiration that streaked through her shirt.

"What do you have?" I asked as I got out of the car.

"Justice," she said, fanning herself with her note pad.

I followed her gaze to a redwood deck attached to a chalet-type house. The deck stood flush against five eucalypts that formed a giant border with the shabby English-style stucco cottage uphill. The decking sparkled in the sunlight. At the near end, wooden chairs painted apple green, lemon, and strawberry clumped around a glass-topped table. At the far corner, the one chaise lounge lay on its side, as if drawing the eye to the gash in the railing above it. A eucalyptus branch that must have been ten feet long and twelve inches in diameter—the assailant presumably—lay nearby. Glancing at the eucalyptus trunks I could see the spot from which the guilty branch had ripped. The bark had already fallen from the trunk, a phenomenon not uncommon in eucalypts. The lines of the scar left by the fallen branch were clear. From where I stood, some thirty feet away, the tear looked rough and abrupt, just as it normally does when a branch tears loose.

"Smith, did the dispatcher tell you who the victim was?"

"No," I said, wiping a hand across my moist forehead.

Pereira's smile widened. "The victim," she said, caressing the word with her voice, "was Hasbrouck Diamond, D.D.S."

"Diamond? I've heard that name. Where?"

"You must never have had this beat—uh, *district*—huh, Smith?" The term "beat" was passé; now beats had become districts.

"No."

"Then you haven't had the pleasure of meeting Leila Sandoval, either?"

"No. Is she Diamond's significant other?"

"You might put it that way," she said portentously. Sweat ran down her forehead into the corners of her eyes and down her cheeks like tears, pale-blue tears. But Connie Pereira didn't seem to notice.

"Pereira! For Chrissakes, it must be a hundred degrees here. In another thirty seconds we're both going to be melted all over the sidewalk."

"Okay, okay. I just wanted to give you the feel of the situation here."

I wiped my hand across the back of my neck. "If the situation is gummy, I think I have the feel."

"Well, Smith, Leila Sandoval lives up there." She indicated the small, heavily cracked, caramel-colored cottage next door. "Diamond and Sandoval had a feud going that would make the Hatfields take note."

The light dawned. "Has-Bitched Diamond! Dr. Hasbrouck Diamond is Has-Bitched!"

Pereira laughed aloud. "You got it. Let me fill you in on the feud," Pereira said, moving under the shade of paperbark tree. "It started with the normal stuff, complaints about overturned garbage cans and cars blocking the driveway. Then Has-Bitched reported Leila Sandoval for working at home without a license. She's a masseuse.

9

She responded by calling us about noise when he had a party. Has-Bitched countered with notifying the zoning commission about her business in her home. She won the hearing but not without weeks of effort. All that hassle seemed to have sapped her. We didn't hear anything for a couple of months. We'd just about decided Has-Bitched had won, when Sandoval delivered a master stroke." Pereira grinned. She shifted her weight onto her right foot and said, "Well, now this one I know only by hearsay. It didn't involve us. The story is that Diamond is crazy about Bev Zagoya. An unrequited passion."

"Bev Zagoya, the mountaineer! I saw her slide show last night, a rather abruptly ended show."

"Good, so you know something about mountaineering then. Well, it seems Sandoval managed to convey to Has-Bitched—God knows how, they're not on speaking terms—that mountaineers are fanatic about perfecting their skills."

I nodded. Bev Zagoya had made that point about skills several times during her detailed description of the preliminaries.

"Sandoval convinced Has-Bitched that mountaineers are always looking for a place to practice rappelling, that it's hard to find a good tall rockface where they can attach their ropes at the top and bounce down without running into ten rock climbers on the way up. So to entice the unresponsive Zagoya, Diamond built, at great expense, a rappelling wall off the far end of his deck."

Despite better intentions, I laughed. "Didn't he know that mountaineers hate to rappel? I know that from one lecture. Bouncing down a hard surface, bound after bound, the chances of turning an ankle or reinjuring a knee . . . Zagoya must have thought he was a fool."

"So the story goes." Pereira wasn't rubbing her hands together, but she looked like she wanted to.

"Sandoval must have loved that. Did Diamond counter?"

Pereira nodded. "He got her good. Seems Sandoval was doing some kind of massage where the clients free their repressed emotions by letting out a healthy scream. But here's the thing about this one, Smith. When Has-Bitched called us to complain, he didn't say a woman was screaming, he said it sounded like there was a wounded cougar in the house next door." Pereira paused. "Smith, you are, of course, familiar with the 'Police Beat' column in the paper?"

I nodded. "Police Beat" with its wry descriptions of our calls—all public record—alternately amused and infuriated us, as the columnist highlighted the most bizarre or absurd cases.

"Well, Diamond admitted later that he had 'Police Beat' in mind when he made the call. But the paper did him one better, it ran the call as their lead. 'COUGAR' HOWLS IN HILLS. According to Sandoval, that story destroyed her business."

I shook my head. "And did she retaliate?"

"If so, it didn't involve us. But I can't believe she didn't, because a couple months later Diamond hit her with City Ordinance fifty-eight seventeen." She paused. When I showed no recognition of the number she said, "Smith, the tree ordinance. Diamond's last complaint was about that eucalyptus. The tree that attacked him!"

Now I did remember. In Berkeley, we take pains to keep the fences of our pasture distant and out of sight. We rarely smack into them. In between those fences, though, we are happy to argue about every weed and pebble. City council meetings last till the wee hours. But many of our municipal wars are over fairness to the underdog.

The tree ordinance, however, was not a battle between haves and have-nots. It was between haves and used-to-haves. Between people who have trees and their neighbors who used to have views. By and large Berkeleyans love trees. On the university campus, gardeners

11

have used giant cranes to transplant sixty-foot Italian stone pines rather than cut them down. Berkeleyans are horrified when lumber companies to the north threaten stands of virgin redwood. But on streets like Panoramic Way, where houses nestle together like toes in a tight shoe and each of those toes sells for half a million dollars, a view of San Francisco Bay, the city skyline, and the Golden Gate Bridge can be a fifty-thousand-dollar eyeful. And a neighbor's redwood that blocks that view is not the same as the virgin redwood a hundred and fifty miles away.

I glanced from the deck to the five eucalypts, and from them to Sandoval's shabby house. "Pereira, Sandoval's not blocking Diamond's view. Her house is uphill from him."

"Not his view, Smith."

"His solar collector?" That was another stipulation of the ordinance—trees that had grown up and blocked a solar collector were liable to trimming, thinning, topping, or removal.

Pereira chuckled. "Only in the most personal sense." Clearly she could barely contain herself. "Maybe Dr. Diamond has spent too much time looking at the jaundiced white of molars. Or the whiter white of dental crowns. But Has-Bitched does not like to see white on his own epidermis. He never said it in the public hearings, of course, but what he wants that sun for is to lie out in it—in the buff. And when that eucalyptus branch attacked, it scraped the tan right off the left flank."

Moving closer to Pereira, I lowered my voice, a tactic that she might have considered. "Pereira, the impression I got from the dispatcher was that the branch just fell on him."

"It seems like it, from the evidence on the branch and the tree where it broke off. You know eucalyptus branches don't bend and creak and ease their way to the ground like some other trees. They break off and—"

"—fall just like that," I said, snapping my fingers before she could get hers in position. "Pereira, I don't call that assault. Assault assumes a perpetrator."

"Ah, Smith"—Pereira moved her hands in a wide arc as if encircling the whole pasture of possibilities—"but, you see, Has-Bitched does call it assault. Has-Bitched says Leila Sandoval hired a tree trimmer to sabotage the branch so it broke off just when he was sitting beneath it."

"How did the tree trimmer manage this feat?"

Pereira laughed. "That Has-Bitched doesn't know. Discovering that, he says, is our problem."

3

RAKSEN, the ID tech, hurried toward me, the bag that held his sampling paraphernalia in one hand, camera case slung over shoulder. He was tall, so thin his pants seemed to stay up by good will alone, and had wiry brown hair and dark eyes that were never still. "Attack of the killer eucalyptus, eh?"

"Raksen," I said, "regardless of what we may think of Diamond and his theory that branches drop by appointment, we have to play this by the book. If he gets it into his head that we're not honoring his complaint he'll be bitching to the Review Commission faster than a eucalyptus branch falls."

"Like that!" he said, snapping his fingers.

I motioned toward the fallen limb. "Go on the assumption that someone managed to sabotage that branch. Check for copper nails, wires, whatever. Cut a cross section. Make a cast. Take photos of the branch end and the spot of the tree it broke from. And let Diamond see that you're giving it the same treatment as you'd give the gun that shot Kennedy."

Raksen nodded impatiently. My entreaty had been

14

unnecessary. Raksen was a perfectionist. He never took one photo when three were possible. When he finished dusting for prints, every surface in the room was covered in powder. No spot was so remote that Raksen would admit a "responsible's" finger could not have been there. He once clinched a case by lifting the guilty UPS man's prints from the inside of the oven door.

"It's the eucalypt at the far end of the deck," I said. "The spot's a good ten feet above the deck. Get it if you can, but don't kill yourself doing it."

Raksen nodded, spun toward the deck and was almost through the hedge before I caught his arm. "And Raksen, ask Diamond for a shot of the injury site. His left flank."

Raksen nodded, and headed toward the branch.

Pereira went to get Diamond. I paused in the shade of the nearest eucalypt just long enough to cool the sweat on my body. That was a mistake, as impulsively grabbed pleasures so often are. (Howard and I had discussed this very issue as we lay in the California King two mornings ago. But we didn't come to the conclusion about mistakes for another hour, when we were within seconds of being late for Detectives' Morning Meeting.)

When I stepped onto Dr. Hasbrouck Diamond's deck the sun felt all the hotter. There was no breeze. Even the sharp, clean smell from the eucalyptus trees beside the deck had lost its edge.

Raksen stood at the far corner, eyeing the tree in question, the overturned chaise lounge and the thick branch beside it. Had the branch broken the railing and rolled off the deck, it could have fallen forty feet to the ground, careened down the hill, and crashed into the house below or anyone who happened to be in the yard. Diamond's neighbor might not have engineered the time of the branch's fall, but if she had weakened the tree, she'd endangered more than Has-Bitched, and this serio-comic feud of theirs was way out of hand.

While Raksen contemplated the angles from which he would photograph, I examined the tree itself. There were no telltale scrapes on the trunk. Like the other four giant eucalypts, it was much too big for the narrow space between the deck and the house next door. A branch or two from each tree extended above the deck. I peered over the deck railing. The ground below dropped off sharply. My throat clutched with panic, a *small* clutch of panic, the residue of a battle with acrophobia. Ignoring that reaction, I stared at the wild shrubs and grass and golden California poppies and poison oak that grew around the bases of the eucalypts. All but the poison oak and the occasional poppy were brown now, victims of the drought year.

But the oddest thing here was the gate in the deck railing, a gate that opened to a forty-foot drop! Swallowing against my tightening throat, I leaned over the railing and looked down. The deck was held up by metal poles anchored in cement bases. Crossbars reinforced them. And beneath me, beneath this odd gate was the rappelling wall Hasbrouck Diamond reputedly had built for his reluctant inamorata. It ran all the way to the ground. And a rope dangled in front of it. A big pasture, indeed, we had here in Berkeley.

Leaving questions about the wall for later, I stood up and looked at Diamond's house. Double sets of glass doors led into the living room. Between them a picture window reflected the eucalypts. The house was a giant shingled shoebox, running lengthwise out over the steep hillside. It was huge for Panoramic Way, where building even a twelve-by-twelve room required drilling steel support poles deep into bedrock. Geranium-filled window boxes lined the edge of the flat roof above the second floor and at the corners curved Chinese-red planks arched pagodalike. From them hung brightly colored sock-flags

16

painted to resemble carp. Today, in the still air, they looked like dead carp.

The glass door opened. The man Pereira shepherded through was probably in his mid-forties, slightly built, with thin light-brown hair and the worst posture I had ever seen on an ambulatory human being. His head jutted forward like a fat carp dangling from the end of a pole. Or the corner of his roof. He gazed down (the only direction he could without difficulty) and with each step he looked in danger of falling forward and tumbling off the deck. Briefly I wondered if the man had some structural deformity, but I remembered someone insisting that Hasbrouck Diamond's appalling stance was due to nothing more than sloppy posture. If so, mothers could have displayed Diamond as a warning to their slouching adolescents.

As I watched Diamond stomp toward me, I recalled one afternoon in Howard's and my office: Jackson, my fellow homicide detective, had been there when Pereira had stalked in from handling the latest Diamond call. "Has-Bitched made his whole complaint staring at his balls," she'd announced.

"Maybe the dude was doing a double-check," Jackson said.

"No need!" Pereira had snapped. "Not after he called and had me make a special trip out there because his neighbor's garbage can spilled on his sidewalk. The guy's got plenty of balls."

Looking at Diamond now, it was hard to say just how tall he might have been. Stooped over he was about my height: five-seven. Even in his face he bore a familial resemblance to one of his carp. His eyes strained forward under the lids. His lips seemed poised to smack together. I had a good view of the top of his head: there was a bald spot there, and pale brown hairs hovered around it. He was wearing a white beach jacket belted loosely over his wrinkled tanned stomach and bathing trunks that covered

17

not enough of his spindly tanned legs. What level of aesthetic self-deception, I wondered, could have led *this* man to exhibit his body nude? Now the sight of his bathing trunks and oiled skin reminded me of the heat, the heat I was enduring in work clothes—because of his complaint. The dichotomy in our dress did nothing to endear him to me. And the implicit condescension of his attire didn't help.

I said, "I'm Detective Smith, Homicide–Felony Assault. Why don't you start from the beginning, Dr. Diamond?"

Most victims balk at repeating their stories over and over again, but Diamond nodded enthusiastically, an action that made his head look all the more like a hooked carp. "That's the branch, right there, Detective. No question it could have killed me. You can see that, right?" He shifted his gaze from the branch to Raksen bending over the end, camera in hand. "She's crazy. I kept telling you people—she's crazy."

It took me a moment to realize Diamond was not anthropomorphizing the eucalypt. I said, "She?"

"My neighbor, Leila Sandoval," he sputtered, thrusting an accusing finger at the cottage beyond the deck rail. He held the pose for effect. But the impression he gave standing there, head down, arm raised to the side, was of a diver about to slip off the end of the board.

I glanced at Pereira, another of those ill-conceived indulgences. She was pressing her lips together to keep from unsuitable behavior. This was not going to be an easy interview for her.

Diamond lowered his arm and raised his gaze. Glaring directly at me, he said, "Detective, the woman's been off the beam for years. She's a lunatic. Ought to be put away."

"Do I understand that you are accusing your neighbor

of breaking off a thick eucalyptus branch ten feet above the spot where you were sitting and dropping it on you?"

"You won't think it's ridiculous when you meet her."

"Now, Dr. Diamond," I said, making an effort to mask any sarcasm, "how do you think she might have managed this attack without alerting you?"

My effort failed; Diamond's flat face reddened. "Officer, I expect service from my police force. This woman has been plaguing me for years and the police have done nothing about it. It's not for lack of my trying, I'll tell you that."

Behind, Diamond Pereira nodded emphatically.

I opened my pad, pushed in the button on the ball-point pen, and waited.

"Look at those branches," he shouted, "they're thick as tree trunks themselves. And hanging out like that, it's no wonder they drop off. She needs to get all those branches trimmed. Any idiot can see that. But do you think she'd do it? Not her."

"So, is it negligence you're talking about?" I asked, lowering my voice in reaction to his.

But that tactic made no impression. Diamond shouted, "Not negligence. Assault!"

"Dr. Diamond, assault and battery assume intent—"

"Of course she intended to hit me. That's why she left the branches like that. She knew there was nothing I could do about them."

I glanced up at the overhanging branches. "I'm sure you know that when a neighbor's tree crosses the property line—"

"They're not over my property line," he muttered, his voice suddenly softer than mine.

"What did you say, Dr. Diamond?"

He dropped his gaze. "Guy who put in my deck," he muttered at his groin, "he built it six feet too wide."

"He built your deck six feet over your neighbor's property?" I asked, struggling to keep my voice even.

Pereira clamped a hand over her mouth. Raksen was lying at the far corner of the deck peering up through his lens, presumably to get the fallen branch and the tree in one shot.

Grabbing back the offensive, Diamond said, "Don't think that lunatic of a woman didn't make hay from that. I was out of town while the carpenter was working. But she was here. If she was as piqued as she made out, she could have stopped him when the first board crossed the line. But not her. She waited till the whole thing was done. Done and stained and waterproofed. Seventeen thousand dollars later. Then she waltzed in here, all smug, and told me I'd have to pull it down. Then the deck would have been no bigger than a sidewalk. It would have been useless. She knew that. And she made hay."

"What specific kind of hay, Dr. Diamond?"

"Twenty thousand dollars. Sheer blackmail," he said to his belt.

"Do you mean she gave you an easement in return for the twenty thousand?"

He nodded, and muttered something to his chest. The only word I could make out was "branches." But that was enough.

"You agreed that the eucalyptus branches can overhang your deck because they are on her property, is that right?"

Flushing to the top of his tonsure, Diamond grunted.

Behind him, Pereira swallowed hard. Her face was nearing the color of his. With considerable effort I restrained a smile of my own as I realized that this was Sandoval's missing thrust in the feud, the one after Diamond's howling cougar. Sandoval had certainly parried in style. No wonder he'd been spurred on to invoke the tree ordinance. "Still—"

"Officer, I lie sunbathing there at the corner of my deck, in my chaise every Thursday afternoon, every sunny weekend. She knows that. Ask Bev Zagoya. She's living here." He looked directly at me, beaming with pride.

"Bev Zagoya, the mountaineer?" I asked, amazed to find she was living here. Had the scorned rappelling wall done the trick after all? Did Hasbrouck Diamond embody an attraction not visible to the naked eye? From what I had seen, Diamond seemed like the last person a woman like Bev Zagoya would choose to live with. "Is she here now?"

"She's taking a break, working on holds up at Indian Rock. She's pitching the Everest expedition tomorrow; we've been working like crazy getting the background data, compiling the figures, hassling the caterers. Tomorrow afternoon the living room will be jammed with money men. Half of Hollywood will be here to get in on the ground floor of the first all-California expedition to Everest led by a woman. That is if that lunatic doesn't sabotage it."

I restrained a sigh. "Do you have some proof she's attempting sabotage?"

"She'd love to sabotage me."

I took that for a no. But I did wonder if Bev Zagoya shared her host's apprehension and if that, perhaps, was the real cause of her peculiar behavior last night. Shifting my attention back to the issue at hand, I said, "Dr. Diamond, did she or anyone else see the branch fall on you?"

"Kris Mouskavachi, one of Bev's associates. He *is* here." He turned, cranking his head up to stare at the tree. "That branch was right over my chair. The lunatic knew that," he insisted angrily. "All she had to do was weaken it. When those eucalyptus branches go, they go like that." His fingers brushed past each other. In the history of eucalyptus, had anyone *ever* described the fall of a branch

21

without attempting to snap his fingers? "Nothing can stop them."

"Dr. Diamond," I said slowly, "since you had these suspicions about your neighbor, didn't it occur to you to sit somewhere else?"

Diamond turned purple. "Move!" he demanded. "Why should I move? It's my deck! That's the one spot where her damned trees don't shade it. I had 'em topped, but look at them!" He shot an arm in their direction. All five eucalypts rose to a point just even with Leila Sandoval's roof, where their tops had been lopped off. New growth poked out from the branches, but that did little to ameliorate the effect of the sawed-off trunks, and, in fact, gave the great trees an unnaturally foreshortened look, rather like Hasbrouck Diamond himself.

"Not two years later and they're already shading out eighty percent of the deck. I'll be damned if that bitch'll make me move out of the sun!"

"Would she be likely to know how you feel?" I asked for form's sake.

"You bet. She knows and she loves it. She's just waiting till the trees shade the whole thing, which'll probably be in another month. Damn trees. Drought doesn't bother them. They grow in heat. They grow in frost. They don't need fertilizer. The damned things are weeds, Detective," he said, dropping his arm and gaze, "sometimes I see her up there looking out the window, just watching those branches grow and block out my sun. I can see her smiling to herself. She's got me by the short hairs."

A clear and present danger for the nude sunbather. I took a deep breath, swallowed hard, and asked, "What exactly gives her this, uh, hold on you?"

"The tree ordinance, Detective. Surely you're familiar with the ordinances of our city."

"But Dr. Diamond, *you* made the complaint about the trees!"

"The damned ordinance is full of holes," he growled. "Twelve point forty-five point oh-four-three gee states that once you've gotten a judgment on a tree you can't get another one for five years. So she's got me for the next three years. Her trees can turn my house into an ice palace and there's not a damned thing I can do."

I jammed my teeth together to keep from laughing. Pereira wasn't so successful. A gurgle escaped her. She made tracks for the far end of the deck. Diamond continued to scowl at his feet.

I swallowed and said, "Dr. Diamond, this is a serious charge you are making. And I have to question Ms. Sandoval's motivation. From what you say, she already had you."

Diamond squeezed his hands into fists. "I keep telling you, the woman's a lunatic. She didn't need a reason. She saw that branch hanging over me and she just couldn't resist it. She's probably up there right now laughing her head off."

"Because the branch fell?"

"Because," he said in obvious exasperation, "she knows I can't sue."

I couldn't help it; I laughed.

"Detective, I obeyed the law!" He glared at me. "I went through the whole process, the way the ordinance instructs. She fought me every step. Of course we couldn't settle the question of those damned trees between the two of us. That woman couldn't agree to walk across the street. So we go to a mediator. Took me six months to find a mediator she'd agree to. Both parties have to agree on the mediator; that's what the ordinance says. This mediator handled the public employees' strike the year before, you remember that. He dealt with the county bureaucracy; he handled ten thousand public employees; but he couldn't put up with Leila Sandoval! He said it was the worst case he'd ever tried. I believe him. The woman's a lunatic!"

Sweat dripped down his shiny face. Wiping a hand across his forehead, he continued. "So we went to binding arbitration. The lunatic agreed to include all five eucalypts in the dispute. The arbitrator's report on the trees said to top 'em. Then, Detective, *she* chose the tree trimmer—that's the law, the tree owner chooses the trimmer, the complainant okays the decision *and* pays for the work. So she chose her trimmer, and probably told him to charge an arm and a leg since *I* had to pay. *And* she must have had him weaken this branch."

I wiped a hand across my own sweaty forehead. "Dr. Diamond, what does all this have to do with her not being able to resist attacking you with a eucalyptus branch and your not being able to sue?"

Diamond leaned over the railing, his face suddenly pale as a deck passenger's at the height of a hurricane. "I had to indemnify her for the cutting. The ordinance says, 'The Complaining Party shall indemnify and hold harmless the Tree Owner with respect to any damages or liability incurred by said owner, arising out of the performance of any work at the behest of the Complaining Party.' So, Detective, if *her* tree falls on me, *I'm* the one who's liable."

HASBROUCK Diamond had not dealt with the question of *how* his neighbor could have engineered the eucalyptus branch to fall at the precise moment he was sitting under it. To him that was a peripheral issue, and after several attempts, all of which led him to new descriptions of his neighbor's villainous character and dearth of sanity, I gave up. I checked out the wound on his left thigh. It was a fairly deep scrape, but hardly of the type that keeps morticians in business. Diamond already had a written report from his doctor. I sent him to get it and his other houseguest, Bev Zagoya's associate.

The man Diamond sent out looked to be about twenty. Despite the heat he wore a long-sleeved rugby shirt and acid-washed jeans. His sun-bleached hair hung an inch below his ears as if he had compromised between the short stylish look, and the long old-Berkeley look. His skin was olive-y enough to have acquired the kind of tan I had spent months working for in the days before the sun had turned into a killer. And his eyes were the pale blue of morning, eyes that foster the illusion of being windows to the soul; they neither moved nervously as Raksen's did, nor did they bulge like Diamond's. What they seemed to be doing was lying back in their wide-apart sockets waiting for another clue to the situation. It took me a moment to realize that he was the blond who'd come into the back of the lecture hall last night at the time Bev Zagoya started rushing her talk.

"Brouck said you wanted to see me," he said. "I'm Kris Mouskavachi. Kris with a K." Hesitantly he extended a hand. On his wrist was a gold watch with a map of Switzerland on its face. The watch was too small for him. It looked more like a woman's watch.

I shook his hand. It was moist. The boy was perspiring, as would be anyone dressed as inappropriately as he.

"Is Kris short for Kristopher? I'll need your full name and address."

Now those eyes narrowed momentarily. "Krishna," he muttered. "Krishna Das Mouskavachi. My address here?"

"And your permanent address."

"I don't have a permanent address. My parents are in Kathmandu."

"Trekking?" Probably ten percent of Berkeley had been to India at one time or another. Maybe a third of those had included Kathmandu, Nepal, in their journeys, some to begin treks through the Himalaya, some to smoke dope unhindered by the exigencies of reality. "Trekking?" I repeated.

Now the boy laughed. All the wariness vanished, and half of his twenty or so years seemed to evaporate. He pulled up the lime-colored chair and plunked himself on the arm. "Trekking! Going to the post office is an expedition for them. And then half the time they forget why they went. They spend days getting ready to go to market, or one of them wanders down five times in an afternoon because their whims change. Trekking!" He laughed again, but there was no bitterness. "You know some of the holy men up there and in Tibet talk about finding pockets in time."

I nodded. I'd heard that before, from the same friend who'd told me about the Buddhist pasture story. A pocket in time was an idea with a lot of appeal. If I had one, I could slide into it, find an apartment, and slide out without losing a minute on this case.

"Well, my parents left here, the States, that is, in 1970. I guess the hippie era, their era, was closing down here then. But they took it with them. And when they got to Kathmandu they didn't just find a pocket in time, they found a pocket with a hole in it. For them it will always be 1970."

"How do they live?"

"Sara, my mother—Sarasvati, but that's not her real name, of course—she inherited some money, and she gets a check every month. There really isn't work in Kathmandu, not for foreigners."

"None? Not in trading or translating?" I asked. I was getting off the track, but there was something about the boy that interested me. Something wasn't quite right, but I didn't have enough information yet to figure out what it was.

"Traders bring their own people. And there are enough Nepalis who speak good enough English. No one needs resident hippies in the middle. Drive and reliability aren't qualities that come to mind when they think of people who've lived in the pocket for twenty years, or grown up in it. You have to be pushy to convince trekkers that they need an intermediary, and that you can do the job." He grinned smugly.

"And you're pushy?"

"Right. I've gone on a few treks with Europeans— over there 'European' includes American. I knew the Nepali porters—not well. Europeans, even hippie Europeans"—he grinned again, but now there was a bitterness

27

in it—"especially hippie Europeans, are always outsiders. The Nepalis have to work like crazy just to survive. There aren't many jobs and they really get riled at the idea of a rich foreigner taking a job that should be theirs. So I could only get on treks where I knew some of the porters and it was clear to them that I wasn't going to be taking the *tsampa* out of their mouths."

Sweat was dripping down my back. Time to rein in my wandering curiosity and get back to the point. "How do you know Bev Zagoya?"

"I was a sort of go-between with the porters on her last expedition."

I eyed him skeptically. I knew the story of Bev Zagoya's last expedition. It was the first mixed-sex assault on one of the Himalayan peaks—I couldn't recall which—to be led by a woman. There had been a lot of fund raising, a lot of celebrating when Bev and some of the others reached the peak. It was over five miles high, in air too thin to support Western lungs. Three climbers—one woman from Minnesota and two Sherpas—had been killed in an avalanche, but that was not uncommon. Climbing was a dangerous sport.

Bev Zagoya had led expeditions before that. She'd had a lot of experience climbing. And in her lecture last night, she had certainly given the impression that she could take care of herself. Novice trekkers might be convinced they needed a resident American teenager as a go-between to deal with the porters, but I couldn't imagine she would have.

I said as much.

A momentary breeze ruffled Kris's blond hair. He leaned closer and lowered his voice. "She should have known, but she was just kind of flustered what with hiring the porters and dealing with the Sherpas, trying to buy enough rice and *tsampa* for everyone and trying to figure out how much gear to give the Sherpas in the beginning and how much to hold back for the time they balk and refuse to go any farther up the mountain unless they get more. They do that. Negotiating from a position of strength, right?" He grinned. "They say that the last climbers gave their Sherpas heavier sweaters, better boots, more cigarettes. There's big confrontation. Lots of drama. I love it. I told Bev I knew the real facts on the last few expeditions. Hiring me was a good decision for her; it probably saved her a couple hundred dollars in gear." He shrugged, but there had been a moment of hesitation before the movement, a moment of consideration. I wondered how conscious Krishna Mouskavachi's charm was.

He wiped a hand across his forehead. "Hot," he muttered. "Want some coffee? There's some iced espresso in the fridge and I can whiz up some milk in the espresso machine. I just love doing it."

On another case I might have hesitated. But now, having foregone breakfast and even my morning coffee, I was hot and tired, too. "Sure."

I followed Kris through Hasbrouck Diamond's glass doors. The living room was wonderfully cool, and white as the Himalaya: white shag carpet, white sofas, white walls, the latter decorated with poster-size photos of white Himalayas, and of views down from those Himalayas onto the variegated green and brown plateaus miles below.

"That's Bev," Kris said, pointing to the tiny red figure at the peak of a summit. "Great photo, isn't it? You can really see the thrill of mountaineering, looking down on the world like a god, standing where no man or at least not many have ever been." He stood staring at the photo. It was, I realized, the first time he had not been watching me, gauging my reaction, and, I was willing to bet, planning his own. He turned back to me, shook his head, and smiled. "Climbers are weird, though. I mean what kind of person risks his life to scale an ice-covered rock? One in ten of them die, you know. That's the average. I've talked to them, the guys I went with and the ones I just saw in the pie shop in Kathmandu—and they'll tell you that there's no high like pitting yourself against the best of nature and coming out on top, no feeling like coming off that exhaustion, still alive even if it's with fingers black with frostbite, your ribs broken, and your toes ready for the amputator's ax. They'll go on and on . . . you get it, don't you?"

"A touch of ego?"

Kris laughed. "More than a touch. A Himalayan share of ego."

"And Bev?"

"The women are no shrinking violets, either, Bev least of all." He made his way around one of the huge white couches. "The kitchen's this way."

I followed him to the street side of the house, into a kitchen that would have made the owners of The Palace take notice. It was long, narrow, and almost as big as my entire former flat on Mr. Kepple's back porch. Its long white counters held every appliance I'd seen and a number whose function I couldn't have guessed. (I'm on the list for every catalog known to man, kitchenware ones included, a testimony to just how indiscriminate mass mailing is.) There was an espresso machine in The Palace, of course, but I had never had time to figure out how to work it. Kris, on the other hand, handled this one like a pro.

"I love Berkeley," he said. "Everyone's so friendly, especially when they find out I grew up in Kathmandu." He pulled a pitcher of coffee out of the refrigerator. The strong coffee aroma filled the room. The pitcher was white, of course. Was Hasbrouck Diamond obsessed with snowy vistas, or was he the least secure home decorator in Berkeley? Carefully, Kris poured the foamy milk atop my coffee. "I know it's not me they're interested in; it could be anyone who'd lived over there. But what the hell, why not enjoy it, right?"

"Don't be so sure it's not you," I said, leaning back against one of the counters. "You're a likable guy." He was. Someone not observing his veneer of bonhomie with a detective's eye might not have noted the moments when he shrank back to check that it was in place. But even watching for the cracks, I couldn't help but like him.

"How'd you end up here, with Dr. Diamond?" I asked as I accepted the proffered glass. I took a drink and felt a jolt of alertness before the coffee hit my stomach.

"Bev told him about me and he offered. He's going to help me with college. I start at Cal in September. I've got a provisional acceptance. They're still trying to evaluate my credits." He flashed a happy grin. "My education hasn't been the most standard. But what he gives me will be a loan," he added quickly. "I'll pay him back when I finish graduate school."

"You're very ambitious," I said, meaning it.

"Compared to my parents? Yeah, I'm the white sheep, all right. Their worst nightmare come true. Their only son leaves the hovel to become a banker, or worse yet the CEO of a Pacific Rim Corporation, and have a house like this."

Hoping to catch him unawares, I said, "And you saw the eucalyptus branch fall on Dr. Diamond?"

Kris poured the steamed milk into his glass with what seemed to be excessive care. "I heard him scream. I was in the TV room, upstairs, so it took me a minute to get down. But the branch was still on top of his leg. He's got a scrape, you know."

I nodded. "How did he seem to you?"

"What do you mean?"

"Emotionally, at that moment?" I meant "Stunned? In shock?" but I didn't want to put words in Kris's mouth.

Now his pale blue eyes, eyes that were clearly not a

31

window to his banker's soul, did move off to one side. I recalled reading somewhere that people do that when they are puzzling something out. He shook his head. "Maybe he was stunned. I've seen people when they've had bad falls. They don't scream and holler right away. It's like the pain hasn't made its way inside yet. Brouck looked like that. He was just sitting there, and he was smiling."

But I had seen that scrape. It wasn't akin to a broken leg in the Himalaya. And I doubted Diamond's smile was due to physical shock. If Leila Sandoval had aimed that branch at him, she had missed. She might even have given him grounds to reverse the decision of the tree arbitrator. I could picture Hasbrouck Diamond smiling as he planned his revenge. To Kris, I said, "Do you know his neighbor Leila Sandoval?"

He glanced through the door into the living room. I followed suit, but there was no telltale sign of Diamond, or anyone else. "Bev introduced me," he said, speaking in even a lower tone. I was bending forward trying to hear him. "But don't tell Brouck. He'd toss me out if he knew."

"How come?" I asked, wanting to get his assessment of the Diamond-Sandoval situation.

He took a long swallow of coffee. "Well, I guess you know about the problem Leila has caused Brouck."

"And Mr. Diamond seems worried about her?" I offered.

He glanced at the doorway and back. "Brouck's a worrier. Sometimes I think Brouck has those flags flying from the roof to ward off Leila, like people do for demons." Kris grinned. "I probably shouldn't tell you this, but then you probably already know it. Brouck's a little obsessed with the idea that Leila's out to get him. He thinks she sits up nights hatching plots."

"And when the tree fell on him?" I prompted.

"It reinforced all his suspicions." Kris hesitated, then put down his glass and leaned toward me. "This is going to sound bizarre. Maybe Brouck's spent too much time with climbers. He can be as weird as they are. The thing is this lecture tomorrow is vital to Bev's expedition. Brouck's invited a lot of Hollywood types with money. He's counting on their support. An American woman leading an Everest climb. It's Hollywood, isn't it?" He grinned.

"So what's Brouck afraid of?"

"He's scared stiff that Leila's off plotting her ultimate revenge, something that will happen in the middle of Bev's lecture."

"What?"

Kris shook his head. "I don't know."

"Something like whatever unnerved her at last night's lecture?"

His eyes narrowed; for a moment he looked like a little boy who had failed. And despite the unusual ease he'd shown with a homicide detective, now he seemed no more mature than any other teenager. He glanced out the dinette window, then back at me. Motioning me into the dinette, he whispered, "It's not fantasy. I was in Leila's house. Brouck doesn't know that. I'd be in trouble if he did. But while I was there she got a call from a beekeeper." He paused, watching for my reaction, clearly expecting more than he got. "Leila had placed an order with the beekeeper for delivery tomorrow." He paused again, and when I didn't respond, he said, "The order, it wasn't for honey."

I shook my head. In normal life this accusation would be too ludicrous to be true. But as an addendum to the eucalyptus attack and the cougar-howling story, it might fit. I could picture Bev's lecture guests swatting bees and stampeding off the deck. And the reporters Diamond would have been sure to invite, writing up the event for laughs. Even so something wasn't right about this story. "And the bees arrive tomorrow?"

Kris grinned smugly. "Not anymore, they won't. I called and canceled the order."

Despite that grin there was still a wariness to his expression. I kept my face unresponsive. Could Leila have been sure a swarm of bees would head from her porch across the deck to Diamond's living room? Even if she had crept onto the deck the middle of the night before and spread honey over it? What would have kept those bees from finding something more appealing uphill?

Kris stood, arms akimbo, watching me.

I shook my head. "Dr. Diamond and his neighbor are pros at getting at each other. I don't believe Ms. Sandoval would go with this bee thing—it's too iffy. Tell me the truth, Kris."

His face tightened, but only momentarily. "Okay," he said, "but I wouldn't have told if you hadn't guessed. I didn't think you would. I guess real cops are smarter than the ones in the movies. Okay, maybe all the bees wouldn't have come this way. Maybe only a few would have gotten inside the living room. But the thing is, Bev's allergic to bee stings. Anaphylactic shock. She could swell up and die if someone didn't give her a shot of adrenaline. If she'd spotted a bee, she'd have been out of here in a flash."

5

LEILA Sandoval, whom I would like to have questioned about both the fallen branch and the bees, was not home. I checked with Knees Bees, the nearest beekeeper. There had indeed been an order to be delivered to Sandoval's address, for one hive and two quarts of honey. Gunther Knees knew Leila Sandoval; they had chatted when she had called in the order. He was ready to swear it had been Sandoval on the phone. The order had been canceled by a young-sounding man Knees didn't know, also on the phone. I asked Knees to hold the order form for us.

I started toward the car. On the deck, Raksen was sawing off the end of the branch. The fresh, pungent odor of eucalyptus filled the still, hot air. I dispatched Pereira to check the base of the responsible eucalyptus. In uniform (serviceable tan slacks, sturdy shoes, thick socks), she was dressed to take on poison oak, I assured her. And when she finished she could move to the more palatable task of doing financial checks on all the principals. Pereira, who viewed the stock market with the same untempered-by-common-sense fascination with which Howard saw his house, had insights and connections in the financial world that amazed the rest of us.

I drove down Panoramic Way, behind campus and across north Berkeley to Indian Rock.

Indian Rock, basically a three-sided pyramid of a boulder with an apex the height of a two-story house, sits between two two-story houses in the north Berkeley hills. It could have a street address. The front face of the rock is almost vertical and to the unschooled like me looks as sheer as a sheet of window glass. But where I saw only smooth surface, three men must have seen steps and knobs and crannies. They were pressing the toes of their sticky rubber rock-climbing shoes against the rough surface, finding toeholds or magically creating them. They dipped hands in what looked like miniature feed bags that hung from their belts in back, arched their fingers and pressed the chalked tips into handholds visible only to them. Not only did they not fall to the ground, they managed to move sideways. And that was not the most amazing thing.

Two of the climbers wore cutoffs and T-shirts, but the third, a novice, had clearly just exited the climbing-gear store, and despite the heat of the day, he was in full dress. His black rubber-soled shoes boasted turquoise sides and red tongues. His shiny tights outlined less than perfect legs with swirls of red, purple, and orange up to one knee, royal blue and green birds to the groin, and two big red roses on the butt. I had time to note each design because the wearer, two feet off the ground, was not moving. He clung to the side of the rock like one of those stuffed cats suctioned onto car windows. Standing near him, a guy in cutoffs and a world-class tan was barking, "Side-cling hold, Stan. Look for the side cling."

Above the clinging Stan, a couple sat atop Indian Rock, drinking Cokes, and dangling sandaled feet over the edge. They, clearly, had ascended by means of the steps cut into the rock. When they finished they would trot down the stairs; Stan, on the other hand, would come down with a thud.

I found Beverly Zagoya on the north face, or more accurately, under it. She was clinging, spiderlike, under the outcropping of rock, not to handholds above it but to minuscule protuberances on the underside. I stood back, leaning against a stone ledge that separated Indian Rock from the house next door, and watched her move to the right, pausing briefly to scan the rock for holds, pressing her whitened fingertips against the stone surface, and following with her feet. A series of white smudges on the rock—like photographic negatives of cat paws in the snow—marked the trail of her hands.

I had seen pictures of Bev Zagoya like the poster of her last expedition in Diamond's living room. Last night at her lecture/slide show she had been narrating mostly in the dark or standing behind a podium looking down at her notes. But now, seeing her close up, I was struck by how much smaller she was than I expected a woman who'd climbed in the Himalaya to be. She wasn't much taller than I, maybe about five eight. Her brown curly hair hung loose a couple of inches below the neck of her red T-shirt. Her firm shoulder muscles and clearly defined thigh and butt muscles set off a tiny waist, giving her the ethereal look of a ballerina rather than a mountaineer.

She reached flat wall and she swung down. I called her name, and when she turned to face me the vision of ethereality vanished. Close up now, I could see that it was the overhanging eyebrows that gave her face its look of plodding determination. Simian. Thick dark eyebrows had done wonders for Brooke Shields, but one look at Beverly Zagoya told me that she had not let her brows grow unmowed for style. They looked like the grass in a freeway median strip in a year when every bond issue had been voted down. Like they should have glasses and a nose attached. They looked like a feature for which I had better find a more acceptable description before I wrote up a report of this interview. "I'm Detective Smith, Homicide–Felony Assault."

"Homicide?"

"*And* Felony Assault. It's about the eucalyptus branch."

She looked back at the rock and shook her head. The multicolored novice was feeling above the overhang for a handhold. When Zagoya turned back to face me her eyebrows had lowered, giving her the look of an unpleasant Neanderthal. "Now you've made me lose my spot! He's going to tie up the rock for half an hour falling on his roses!"

"We should be done in half an hour," I said as reasonably as I could muster.

"Sunday climbers!" she muttered loud enough for Rose Butt to hear. Then she stomped to the ledge and settled beside me in the filmy shade of a live oak.

"Indian Rock is a safe spot. Where else are people going to start?" I said, more righteously than someone who had just been comparing her eyebrows to a median strip had any business doing. Opening my note pad, I said, "You're a friend of both Hasbrouck Diamond and Leila Sandoval, right?"

Zagoya was still looking toward the rock. Her right foot was poised on its toes, the muscles of that leg taut, as if ready to sprint forward and knock Rose Butt off the bulge on which he appeared to have impaled himself. He lay on the top, arms and legs spreadeagled so that even if he had holds he was too splayed out to pull them off. I started to rephrase my question, when Zagoya said, "Leila introduced me to Hasbrouck, way before their squabble. Three or four years ago. Anyway, Leila and I weren't really friends. She was just someone I met here one day. She was trying the rock."

"Leila climbs?"

"She gave up after a month. Look, the thing with Leila is she's flightly. She can't stick to anything."

"What else has she abandoned?"

Zagoya shook her head. "I really don't know her anymore. But look how she got carried away with this feud with Hasbrouck and all her harassing. She's even called you guys, right?" Zagoya didn't wait for an answer. "But she did do one good thing that will have a long-range effect." Now she did wait till I dutifully asked what. "She introduced me to Hasbrouck, and Hasbrouck has become a real supporter of mountaineering. He's going to do it a lot of good."

"Like?"

"Like bringing Kris Mouskavachi over here. Kris is going to be a big plus for mountaineering. Like organizing my presentation for the expedition. Like underwriting the filming. He's invited a lot of influential people tomorrow. Some media. We need to have the public know what goes into mountaineering, that it's not just trotting up the Himalaya while Sherpas or Hunzas carry your tent."

"Were you worried about your lecture last night or the presentation tomorrow?"

She tensed slightly, then shook her head. "I leave the worrying to Hasbrouck."

"Does Hasbrouck Diamond climb, too?"

"No. He's smart enough to realize he's in no shape for it, not even rock climbing."

"*Even* rock climbing?" I asked, amazed.

She turned toward me. The brows lifted. And I had the sense that she had shifted into her public persona. "I don't mean to suggest that rock climbing doesn't take a lot of skill. You've got to be in good shape for class-five or better climbing." Watching my reaction, she added, "A class-five slope is one that is dangerous enough that a fall could kill you, one that most climbers should use support on. Above that you'll have to put your full weight on the rope, and you'll find yourself hanging from your harness and swami belt," she said, touching a two-inch-wide sash that had been circled four times around her waist and knotted.

When my expression still didn't satisfy her, she lowered the brows a millimeter—unintentionally, I guessed—and said, "Climbs are graded. Class one is a sidewalk, flat and easy. When you go to the store you're doing class one. Class two is a slope, maybe tree roots or debris on it. No harder than walking down a dune to the beach." She smiled automatically. What she was giving me was a line from her public presentations. I could feel my neck tighten. It was ridiculous, but I was insulted. Cops do not feel insulted when interviewing. I couldn't decide whether I was put off by her rote delivery, or by her assumption that I didn't realize it for what it was. But I did know this wasn't the time to ponder *that*. "Class three's a steep slope, which you can manage without equipment, but you should keep a rope handy if you're not experienced. For four—"

"Where were you when the eucalyptus branch fell?"

The deep creases in her forehead exposed her anger at the interruption, or the wresting of control. I wished I knew just how much experience she had doing public presentations. Probably more than her public demeanor suggested. Either that or she was more nervous about her appearances than she was willing to let on. Of course, she would have had good reason to be worried about tomorrow's presentation.

"I was downstairs," she said, her voice revealing nothing. "My room is beneath the main floor. I heard the bang when the branch dropped. I ran upstairs. Hasbrouck was still in the chair."

"Did you look up in the tree?"

"Of course, but if you're asking was there anyone

there with a chain saw, the answer is no. No saws, no ropes, no felonious woodpeckers," she said, exasperated. "Look, I know Hasbrouck thinks Leila had it in for him. Maybe she did, maybe she still does. She's a middle-aged woman with nothing to do with her life; she has a lot of time to nurse a silly vendetta. But there's no way she could engineer a ten-foot eucalyptus branch to fall at the time Hasbrouck was out airing his parts."

In front of us there was a thud, followed by a yelp. The novice climber had landed on his roses. Before he could push himself up and dust off his colors, Bev Zagoya was up and at the rock.

I walked up next to her before she could get her foot planted. Even if I hadn't had a question, I wouldn't have let her decide when the interview was over. "One more question," I said, pausing long enough to make my point. "Are you allergic to bees?"

She turned around. "Why?"

"Are you?"

She glanced around nervously, moved a step farther from the climbers on the rock before she spit out, "Yeah, I am. So?"

"Why are you loath to admit it?"

Again she seemed to struggle with herself before answering. It was a power thing, I was willing to bet. "Look, I'm in a very competitive sport, a business in a sense. Any weakness makes me less salable," she said, her voice lower. "And it means I have to work that much harder. So I don't want this spread around."

"Does Leila Sandoval know about it?"

I could see the fear taking hold as she nodded and said, "Why are you asking?"

"Because Leila Sandoval ordered bees to be delivered to her address tomorrow."

She slammed her fists together. Leila Sandoval was fortunate not to be between them. "Tomorrow!" She slammed the fists harder. "God damn her!" Another slam. Her face was crimson under the tan, and all her muscles were taut.

Another person might have reacted to the physical danger of anaphylactic shock, the possibility of her own tissues swelling up till they blocked off the oxygen and suffocated her. But clearly, Bev Zagoya was focused on the threat to her presentation. It was a statement of her commitment, and of her priorities. I waited a moment, then motioned her back to the stone wall we'd been sitting on and said, "Now tell me what's behind this bee order."

"Leila's a lunatic—"

"I already heard that from Dr. Diamond. Why the bees? Why tomorrow?"

"To destroy me. Destroy my chance to get backing for my expedition. Look," she said glaring at me, "no one's going to be interested in filming a climb led by a woman they've seen running away from an insect. It's hardly heroic, is it? You satisfied now?" Her face was even redder.

"Would you be in danger climbing? You could carry adrenaline."

"I do. Chances of me getting stung when I can't get to it are slim. I know that, but try to convince the backers. Backers aren't charities, you know. What they want to make is an adventure film in which they themselves take no chances, however remote. Suppose I was stung on the way to the mountain, in some squalid, unphotogenic location. It would ruin their story line. More to the point, if these guys saw my presentation ruined by a swarm of bees, they'd start viewing the whole project differently. Instead of an epic, in their minds it'd be Laurel and Hardy."

I sighed. My shirt was sticking to my back and my hair felt clammy against my scalp. On the wall in front Rose Butt had reclaimed Bev's spot and was peering around for holds; Bev gave no sign of noticing. I said, "So this bee issue is a devastating threat. Why would your old friend Leila Sandoval do this to you?"

She gave a little snort of disgust. "Because of Hasbrouck."

I sighed; Diamond, of course. Diamond and Sandoval must have the biggest blinders in the entire pasture. They would not only not see the fence, they wouldn't see the knolls, the streams, or the other horses. They would see nothing but each other. "To get to him, because he's your friend?"

She looked down at the path, and I had the feeling she could hardly make herself go on. "Because," she forced out, "Hasbrouck is, well, enamored of me. He loves being part of the climbing world, but he came to that love because I love it, and because"—she swallowed— "because Hasbrouck loves me. I don't encourage that," she said quickly, "but I can't help how he feels, can I?"

I could have commented that staying in Diamond's house was not an act likely to dim his ardor. Instead I studied Zagoya. There was no pretense in her humiliation. Her face was nearly as red as it had been in anger. But all that seemed an excessive reaction for one who denied her own involvement in this infatuation. I said, "I have the feeling you're protesting too much."

She didn't reply, but the tightening of her body told me I was right.

"Let me remind you," I said, "that you are dealing with the police. You have been threatened; I'm trying to protect you. And I'm also getting fed up with having to pull the truth out of you." I paused to let the unspoken threat sink in. "Why is it that Leila Sandoval would aim to harm you because Diamond is attracted to you?"

She didn't reply.

Atop the rock, the couple sitting there laughed. I looked up in time to see them kiss. The memory of

Howard's kiss as he hoisted himself out of bed this morning flitted through my mind, followed by a pang of disappointment at our lost day. I looked back at Bev, and suddenly I saw a possibility I hadn't considered, which seemed hardly imaginable. A soap opera possibility. "There's a lid for every pot," my mother had said, an unintentionally backhanded compliment when an amply endowed cousin had announced her engagement. To Bev Zagoya I said, "Leila introduced you to Diamond. And Diamond turned his attention to you. Was Hasbrouck Diamond involved with Leila Sandoval before?"

Beverly Zagoya nodded.

"Are you sure?" I demanded, still hardly able to imagine it.

"Oh, yeah. I'm sure. She told me. That's why her husband left her."

There was no way I could ask Bev Zagoya the questions I most wanted to: How could any woman be attracted to Hasbrouck Diamond? How awful must Leila Sandoval's husband have been for her to find Diamond preferable? How insulting had that betrayal been for Mr. Sandoval?

Bev Zagoya must have asked herself the same questions at one time, for while I was still discarding the unutterable inquiries, she said, "Their affair began seven or eight years ago. Leila told me Brouck didn't look so bad then."

I didn't allow myself to mutter a knowing "Uh-huh." Instead, I said, "Leila's not at home. Where can I find her?"

Clearly relieved at my change of focus, she said, "On Telegraph. She's a masseuse. And she's got a space there on the Avenue."

"She's rented an office there?"

"No, she's got a blanket on the sidewalk."

"Are you sure?"

"Oh, yeah. No one wants you to get her more than me."

"Doing massage?"

"Yeah," she said in disgust, "she's a classic case of Berkeley syndrome."

6

I HEADED for Telegraph Avenue and the sidewalk massage "parlor" I could hardly believe was there. Before my promotion, I had been beat officer on the Avenue, where street artists' displays lined the sidewalks. The pasture fence was barely visible at all there. But even on Telegraph the city fathers did not allow bare buns to be rubbed.

As I drove downhill I thought about Leila Sandoval and Berkeley syndrome. Maybe I should have guessed it about her, but syndromees were not usually found in such posh addresses as Panoramic Way.

Like the street artists on the Avenue, Berkeley syndrome was a phenomenon that flourished here. Many Berkeleyans had come to town as students. Caught by political awareness, social concern, or artistic aspiration combined with disdain for material possessions, they had stayed. After graduating, or dropping out, they had worked for the good of their fellow man, or they'd followed their muse, sitting in the warm sunshine of commitment. They had stored good karma against the chill of a middle age they were sure would never find them. They worked twenty hours a week to pay the rent, but they knew they were not insurance or real estate agents; they were union organizers or metal sculptors. And, in Berkeley, everyone else knew that too. They were not ne'er-do-wells as they would have been back East, they were people "who'd gotten their priorities straight."

Berkeley syndrome had blossomed in the Sixties, and bloomed well through the Seventies. By the mid-Eighties, the syndromees were well into their forties. Eyes that had peered into blocks of stone and seen visions of beauty now needed bifocals; teeth that had chewed over the Peace and Freedom platform required gold crowns that part-time jobs would not pay for. And the penniless life with one change of jeans and a sleeping bag to unroll on some friend's floor was no longer viable. The need of a steady income became undeniable. And so they scraped together the money, took a course in accupressure, herbalism, or massage, and prepared to be responsible adults. Rarely did massage or the like support them. Berkeley is not L.A., where hyperactive moguls need daily rubdowns. Here a weekly massage, to calm the unenlightened spirit, is a luxury. And there are not enough of those luxuries to support the number of nimble fingers in the city. I wondered if massage students like Leila Sandoval really expected to support themselves, or if the time spent in massage classes was just a more subtle show of Berkeley syndrome.

I had a vague picture of what the syndromee would look like: in her mid-forties, with shoulder-length graying hair, no makeup, or makeup so immaturely applied that none would have been preferable—all in all, a woman so laid back that life had not noticed her. And, I thought as I turned onto Telegraph, that was not a look that would stand out on the Avenue.

I wiped the perspiration from my forehead and laughed. The picture I had of Leila Sandoval was, of course, the stereotype, and only one of the many the

47

syndromee could fit. I could as easily have pictured Murakawa, who planned to reapply to physical therapy school *next year*. Always next year. Or someone who had spent the last two years sleeping in a bag on Mr. Kepple's back porch, someone who still couldn't find the time to go out and rent a real apartment. Leila Sandoval could look too much like me for comfort.

It was nearly three in the afternoon when I parked the car near Cody's Bookstore and started up the Avenue.

Although it was Friday, on the Avenue it looked like a Saturday. Street artists lined the three blocks between here and the Cal campus, a veritable convention of syndromees. Between their display cases and card tables and the crowds of browsers, the sidewalks were nearly impassable. Everyone who had not taken the day off to drive across San Francisco to the beach, or to go sailing on the Bay, was ambling along peering at displays of mushroom-shaped candles, beaded earrings, or a table of T-shirts with maps of Ireland, the Tarot magician, the periodic table, and "Berkeleum, atomic number 97, atomic weight 248?" Tanned summer school students in shorts mixed with former students of all ages dressed, as Pereira had once commented "as if they were going to a costume party representing their favorite year."

The Avenue had been gentrified recently, with copy shops replacing head shops and clothing chains where the Indian import shops used to be. But some things hadn't changed, or at least had reemerged. There were displays of necklaces made from pounded silver spoons, key rings from forks, Jockey shorts decorated with what appeared to be finger paints. And tie-dye! Tie-dyed T-shirts, dresses, shorts, tights, tablecloths. The entire length of the street could have been carpeted in the tie-dyed clothing hanging from the display racks beside it.

I was halfway across Durant when I spotted Kris Mouskavachi, rising from a squatting position where he had been talking to a woman sitting on a carpet on the sidewalk. I made my way through the crowd toward him and was within ten feet when I realized this was not Kris Mouskavachi at all, but a blond in cutoffs who could almost have been Kris. This boy was bare-chested with a tattoo of a graceful Monterey cypress that covered his entire back. He made his way purposefully through the crowd coming down Durant toward Telegraph, and walked up to a man in a yellow-banded Panama hat. As he stopped to talk to him he turned, and I had a view of his chest. The tattoo extended over his shoulders like a shawl. Close up, I realized, this boy was older, taller, and had none of the future CEO look Kris did. And the man to whom he was talking was the last person a CEO would "interface with": Herman Ott, the private detective.

Ott's aversion to the Establishment (police, in particular) was well known, though occasionally I had been able to squeeze some information out of him—with the same effort it might have taken to squeeze out an egg before laying time. And the lubricant of money from the discretionary fund. At this moment I owed Ott seventy dollars (it seemed I always owed him). I walked on across the street, comforted in the knowledge that no matter how much Ott wanted to nag me about his money (it was three weeks overdue; he'd already called me twice) he wasn't about to do it on the street.

I passed within three feet of Ott. From under his Panama hat he glared. I couldn't restrain a smug grin. I'd pay for that the next time I needed something from Ott. Herman Ott had many things, but a sense of humor was not among them.

It was near the corner there just a few feet up Durant in a shady spot that I spotted Leila Sandoval. As it turned out, both Bev Zagoya and I were right. Although the city fathers did not allow restorative treatment for bare derrières, Sandoval was indeed plying her trade here. Her sign said FOOT MASSAGE! Bare *feet* we did allow.

The whole foot-massage arrangement looked like something out of the Casbah. A bearded man in safari shorts and a Florida shirt sat on one of those woven plastic beach chairs with a seat just high enough to keep the flesh off the ground. Both his legs were stretched out across a cotton Oriental rug, and one foot lay enthroned on a padded stool. Sitting cross-legged, with the foot cupped in her hands, was a large woman in drawstring pants, with graying curly hair hanging down onto a black T-shirt. The back of the shirt was decorated with a white outline of the sole of a foot with a lot of white circles drawn on it, most of them filled with illegible words. It looked like an illustration for athlete's foot. She was the woman to whom the tattooed Kris Mouskavachi clone had been talking.

Bending over her I asked, "Are you Leila Sandoval?"

She leaned closer to the foot in her lap, staring at it as a fortuneteller might at a crystal ball. "Hmm. This treatment will take another fifteen minutes. One is scheduled afterward. I can take you at four," she said without looking up.

"Detective Smith, Berkeley Police. I need to talk to you about the eucalyptus branch—"

She laughed. Giving the foot a friendly pat, she turned to me. "Has Has-Bitched called you about that? I suppose he thinks I have power over trees. Can't it wait, Officer?"

"And the bees," I added.

She looked up, startled. Her face, which I had imagined in my Berkeley syndrome picture as being devoid of makeup, was a collage of colors: bright pink lipstick, black-outlined eyes with turquoise lids, and circles of rouge on either cheek. Had she been blond she could have passed for a middle-aged Kewpie doll. A nervous Kewpie.

Looking down at her, I realized that she was not a

large woman, as I had first thought, but really rather small, with very well-muscled shoulders and arms, the type of shoulders and arms capable of supporting fingers that dug into feet hour after hour. Or haul her up a eucalyptus. She reminded me of a marmot, one of those little pointy-faced animals with teeth sharp enough to tear into a hound.

A couple stopped beside us, staring from me to Sandoval, to the customer in front of her. The customer looked with horror at his foot as if it were about to be held hostage.

"This is my livelihood," Sandoval insisted to me.

The couple, now joined by another pair, murmured in support.

"If you know about Has-Bitched," Sandoval said, pressing her advantage, "you know he's forced me out of my house. Onto the street. This is the only place I can work."

There was a shrill note of desperation in her voice. As I looked down at her I wondered if that fear was of me or of her uncertain future, if she had yet reached the stage of Berkeley syndrome in which she had to face the truth that foot massage—this last, desperate hedge against reality— was not going to support her, that she would have to abandon her dream for the drudgery of eight to five, to sell the next ten to twenty years of her life so she wouldn't have to spend the remaining ones begging for spare change.

Or, if having ordered the bees that could have endangered Bev Zagoya's life, she expected Diamond to make the next move. Perhaps, then, she had good reason to be afraid.

The crowd was growing. In it I recognized two familiar faces, agitators of nearly professional status. It was a perfect setup for them—hot, crowded, late enough so spectators had plenty of free time.

"I only need fifteen minutes," Sandoval said. "I can't leave this treatment half done." Looking down at the foot in her hands she added, "There are still toxins in his system."

The crowd murmured.

I glanced around, hoping for a glimpse of a patrol car or one of the walking officers.

"What's fifteen minutes?" a voice demanded. "The city of Berkeley would support that concession. Have a cup of iced coffee while you wait—on me!"

I looked at the speaker with amazement, not because of his words, but because the man who had spoken them was Herman Ott. Herman Ott speaking to a cop in public! Herman Ott offering to pay for something!—albeit in a situation where I could hardly accept.

"She's just trying to earn a living," Ott insisted. Ott was smiling. He was paying me back sooner than I'd expected.

The crowd had grown to nearly two dozen. I had a featured role here in what was turning into the best show on the Avenue. This was neither the time nor the place for a confrontation. Even Leila Sandoval's having ordered the bees gave me no grounds for arrest. To her I said, "Okay, finish up."

Ott sidled up, took my arm, and headed toward the corner. "Good save," he muttered.

"You understand," I muttered back, "that the price of coffee, a *latte*, comes out of your seventy bucks."

"It was worth it."

"Sandoval a client of yours?" I asked.

But that was the end of Ott's *glasnost*. He dropped my arm, muttered something inaudible, and stomped off into the crowd. I was tempted to go after him, but in the long run this public show of familiarity wouldn't do me any good either. Instead I turned and started back toward Sandoval's blanket.

Leila Sandoval's spot was fifteen feet away. The beach chair sat atop the Oriental rug—empty. And Leila Sandoval was gone.

The crowd of spectators had dispersed. I questioned the braided-bracelet maker on one side of Sandoval's blanket, and the stained-glass-panel seller on the other. Both insisted they'd been occupied with their own customers. They hadn't realized Sandoval was gone.

I ran into the nearest stores, but there was no sign of her. I was spinning my wheels here. For an Avenue regular there are plenty of bolt-holes. Like as not, Leila Sandoval was peering out of one of them watching me. Like as not, half an hour after I left she would be back on her blanket rubbing another foot. I made a show of leaving the corner, striding across the street against the light, forcing two cars to squeal to a halt. I hurried on through the slow-moving crowd to the patrol car. Sweat was dripping down my back by the time I pulled open the door and reached for the radio mike to call the dispatcher.

"Five twenty-seven," I said, announcing my badge number. I gave him Leila Sandoval's description. He would notify the walking officers on the Avenue. Then I drove around the block, left the car on Bowditch, walked up Durant halfway to Telegraph, cut down a driveway, and went in through the never locked back door of Herman Ott's building.

I raced up the two flights of stairs in the old office building. The hallway formed a square with the offices-cum-apartments on the outside and old-fashioned bathrooms with separate rooms for toilet and sink on the inside. The once fashionable building had gone downhill. By the Seventies Herman Ott was the most respectable businessman here. The "offices" had been converted—informally—to cheap apartments. But in recent years things had taken an upturn. Refugee families had moved in while they adjusted to American life. Usually the apartment doors were open and the smells of coconut sauce or curry filled the hallway. Usually toddlers on bicycles raced around corners. Now the doors were shut and the hall empty. It must have been a hundred degrees in here. Panting, I ran to the end and pounded on the milk glass panel that said HERMAN OTT DETECTIVE AGENCY. No answer. I hit the o harder. Maybe that was good therapy. There was no other benefit. Briefly I considered knocking on the closed doors down the hall. But in this building Herman Ott was a hero, a man who helped his neighbors through the mystifying bureaucracies. If Ott was avoiding me, I wouldn't have expected his neighbors to help me out.

Still fuming I walked down the stairs, telling myself that patrol would find Sandoval. At this very moment an officer would be checking her house, and walking officers would be questioning street vendors near Sandoval's abandoned space. The best thing for me to do would be to go back to the station and wait. I had plenty of paperwork. There were thirty-seven assault cases on my desk to finish processing. Tomorrow I had a hearing for a warrant; there were still two officer's reports I needed to round up for that. Before I got those, patrol would have Leila Sandoval waiting for me.

I thought wistfully of my lost day. I had planned to spend it with Howard, looking at a few apartments, then a swim, a bottle of wine on one of The Palace decks, maybe a dip in the hot tub if the weather cooled, and a long, lovely evening that would meander like a teasing finger into a long, lovely night.

A long, lovely fantasy.

At least, I told myself, as I headed back to the station, this day was already shot. It couldn't get worse.

But when I got to the station, I found I'd been wrong.

THE Berkeley Police Station was built by the WPA during the Depression. It is a four-story rectangle. The front desk and the row of chairs on which civilians wait is on the second floor. But to get there, civilians enter through a plain stucco room on the ground floor, a room that holds nothing but a work table and a pile of public-service notices. And the fey touch of a split curving staircase, à la *Gone With the Wind*, hugging either wall.

I climbed to the third floor and pulled open the door of the tiny office I shared with Howard, a room that was definitely not Tara quality. The only similarity might have been the temperature. It must have been a hundred degrees in there, too. The papers in my IN box drooped limply over the sides of the box. Without looking at them I went downstairs to Files and ran the names of Leila Sandoval, Hasbrouck Diamond, and Krishna Das Mouskavachi through PIN for outstanding warrants, CORPUS for arrests. No warrants, no arrests, none for any of them.

Then, assuring myself that this day had already provided me its quotient of frustration, that it was almost over, that in an hour I could still meet Howard at the pool for lap swimming, I made my way back to the office and sat down at my desk to tackle my IN box. On top was a note from Murakawa, reminding me I'd promised to talk to Mr. Kepple about his neighbors' complaints. So much for self-proclaimed assurances. In the pasture the spot Mr. Kepple occupied was the one all the flies buzz around. For obvious reasons. Trying to rein him in there would make a fitting end to my day.

Or so I thought until I read the next message: Inspector Doyle was in his office, waiting for me.

Our pasture fence may be barely visible most places, but where Inspector Doyle is, you can see every board and every nail.

"Go on in, Smith," the officer outside his door said. There was a funereal quality to his voice. There was *always* that funereal quality. Most times it was warranted. Inspector Doyle was not known for his patience or good humor. I had seen him laugh once or twice, but neither of those times had been during this calendar year.

Inspector Doyle nodded at me as I opened his office door. His once red hair had thinned and was mixed with gray. He reminded me of an old red hound lying in the dust, the folds of his neck quivering as he panted heavy old-dog breaths and peered out under sagging eyelids to watch a small terrier prance by. Then in one motion he'd spring forward and snap his teeth around the terrier's neck.

On the seat to the left of the door sat Raksen, the ID tech, looking exactly like that terrier.

"I can come back when you two are done, Inspector," I said hopefully.

But that escape wasn't to be. "Sit down, Smith."

I sat. And watched. I had worked under Inspector Doyle for over a year, paired *with* him on murder cases, sat in this chair talking strategy, called him at home when a break came, shared the satisfaction of marking a manila

56

jacket *Closed*. I still couldn't ward off his thrusts, but I had learned the rhythm of his reactions and I could see those thrusts coming.

Inspector Doyle leaned forward on his desk. Piles of papers squirted out from under his elbows. "What is it about you, Smith? What do you do to these people? I've got two other Homicide–Felony Assault detectives; no one's calling complaining about them."

I shot a glance at Raksen. His normally pale face was ashen. His fingers were white against the manila folder on his lap. He looked like a terrier Doyle had not just snapped at, but mangled, spit out, and left on the ground a week ago.

Doyle inhaled a long, labored breath. "Now what do you make of this, Raksen? Smith goes out on a simple assault call. Nothing undercover, right? The victim was stark naked at the time of the attack."

"So he said," Raksen muttered. I could almost see the old yellowed teeth grazing Raksen's terrierlike neck. And yet Doyle's rhythm was off. I had seen him go for flesh often enough, but he didn't do it without a buildup.

"The two of you, you've got the victim, you've got the weapon right in front of you. And in less than four hours we've got the victim complaining about incompetence."

"Incompetence?" I said before I could catch myself. I was prepared for Doyle to light into me about the fiasco on Telegraph, but not for *Diamond* talking about incompetence. It was too soon for him to have heard about Sandoval's escape. "About what? I took his statement. I interviewed both his house guests. I attempted to interview his neighbor." I did not bring up her departure. "Raksen took a mold of the eucalyptus branch—"

"And didn't notice the wound," Doyle snapped.

"Wound?" I looked at Raksen. We'd both checked Diamond's leg. There had been no broken skin, no black, blue, or yellow marks. Only the scrapes from the falling eucalyptus branch.

"Wound on the crotch," the inspector went on.

"He didn't tell *me* that," I said. "And I didn't check there." From all I had learned of Leila Sandoval, that did seem the type of wound she might have felt driven to inflict. Damn the woman for escaping me. Damn me for letting her. I could picture her kicking Diamond in the balls, but still couldn't see how she could have managed to get a eucalyptus to do it.

"Diamond said there was a wound, a depression, that had been dug into the crotch of the tree—"

"The crotch of the *tree!*"

"That's where the branch comes into the trunk, Smith." Doyle's cheeks quivered; he was as close to laughing as he'd been this year. He fought it back.

"Dug in? There was a depression, but there was no sign of fresh digging, was there, Raksen?" I asked.

Before Raksen could respond, not that he looked likely to, the inspector continued. "Not new, maybe a year old. And in that wound there were bacteria."

"So that branch was weakened," I said. "They say eucalyptus branches fall without warning. I guess bacterial wounds are one of the reasons why."

"And do you know why those bacteria were able to survive, Smith?" Doyle didn't wait for a reply. "Because water had collected in that wound."

"Water?"

"In August of a drought year, Smith."

"The wound was wet," Raksen muttered.

Despite all my experience with Inspector Doyle, I laughed. "Inspector, what we've got here is a soap opera. Sandoval left her husband for Diamond, hard as that is to imagine. Diamond tossed her aside for Bev Zagoya. Sandoval may well be bitter. She did order a hive of bees, most likely to disrupt the presentation at his house tomorrow. But gouging out a hole ten feet above his deck and tossing in bacteria, I find that a bit hard to believe. And now is he asking us to believe she watered that hole every week like a goddamned houseplant?"

Doyle's face colored. Out of the side of my eye I could see that Raksen was paler. I should have stopped then. I didn't. "How did Diamond say Sandoval did the watering? Did she shinny up the trunk every Sunday morning when he wasn't looking? Or did she hang a hose out her window?"

The inspector jammed his teeth together. His face got redder. "You think that's funny, do you, Smith?"

Maybe it was the result of letting Leila Sandoval outsmart me. Maybe I was just tired. I should have kept my mouth shut, but I didn't. "It's ludicrous. I'm sick of us running out to deal with Diamond and Sandoval and their prepubescent squabble."

"Smith, you're a public servant. You don't get to choose which citizens deserve your time. You're paid to serve them all. You understand that?"

"Inspector, I have served Diamond. We all have. On this he's had a patrol officer, a homicide detective, and an ID tech. We don't normally send out ID techs for fallen branches. The man's not getting his money's worth, he's getting the jackpot."

I expected Doyle's teeth to plunge well into my jugular. But his only reaction was the deepening red of his face, and the tight set of his jaw. He rapped a finger on the desk. Unbalanced piles of papers jerked in response. "Smith," he said slowly, "I know about Has-Bitched Diamond. I know about his feud with Leila Sandoval, and I know about the tree controversy. I know the man is a pain in the ass."

I nodded, amazed at his control. Amazed and wary.

"By rights we should be able to file this complaint under loony."

I nodded again. Raksen sat back. I didn't.

"But if you think this is a joke, Smith, you're missing the ball. Diamond's a pain all right, but he's a dangerous pain. He's already called me once, to say he's getting slipshod service here."

"He knows better."

Undaunted, he continued. "That call, Smith. It came on my private line."

I was beginning to see the ball now. It was sailing over my head. "Diamond has your private number?" I said. "Who else's number does he have?"

For the first time, Doyle nodded. "Exactly, Smith. You got that, Raksen?"

Raksen looked paler yet. Clearly, he didn't get it. In the lab Raksen was the best, but his real love was for microbes. In his view, man's role was as host.

"How long do you think it'll be, Raksen," Doyle asked, as if to a dim child, "before Diamond's on the horn to the chief, the mayor, the papers?"

"But, Inspector," Raksen said, "they must know what he's like, too."

Before Doyle could position his teeth, I said, "All the better for them."

But Doyle wasn't deterred. "Raksen," he said, staring straight at me, "you must still think news reporting is merely passing on the truth. The truth is that August is a slow news month. Everyone, except Diamond, dammit, is on vacation. It's too late for floods, too early for hurricanes, too warm to bemoan the plight of the homeless. The city council's on vacation, the students haven't returned. Nothing is happening. There is no news, Raksen. Nothing to sell newspapers. You got that? And then, Raksen, Hasbrouck Diamond bursts onto the scene, bitching that his bare flank was attacked by a eucalyptus. It's a gift from the gods, Raksen. With a clever headline—"

"LIMBS ATTACK LIMB." It got out before I could stop myself.

"When they find that Diamond is accusing his neighbor of using a tree limb to maim or kill him—"

"BRANCH OFF TO ETERNITY."

"And when they find out that the crotch of the tree was wet . . ." He paused.

I could read the dare in his eyes. I couldn't resist. "'WET CAVITY FELLS DENTIST.' We're talking family papers, Inspector."

Doyle flashed a smile. It only served to make the glower that followed darker. "You've got the game, Smith, so tell Raksen here what happens when they get the report that Diamond is complaining about us."

"'COPS FINGER CROTCH WHILE MASSEUSE RUNS LOOSE.'"

Back in my office, I called the dispatcher three times, even though I knew he would have contacted me as soon as he heard from patrol. Leila Sandoval should have ambled back to her Oriental rug and beach chair on the Avenue an hour ago. The longer she was absent, the more uneasy it made me. There was nothing I could do. I couldn't get a warrant for her; as it stood now I didn't even have grounds to charge her. You can't charge a woman because her tree branch falls, or because she chooses to purchase a beehive.

I had been flippant with Inspector Doyle, no doubt about that. It was as if I had peeled off the thickened top layer of chocolate pudding and tossed it on the table between us. And now, I was left with just the pudding beneath, the mushy pudding of apprehension.

8

AS I HEADED across the parking lot to my car, Raksen was starting up his old brown Dodge. He backed up and sat in the lane for a moment staring at me, then pulled up next to me. His face was still as pasty as it had been in Doyle's office. A film of sweat covered it and coated his wiry hair. He looked like a terrier who'd just been hauled out of the sink by the scruff of the neck. "Two things, Smith," he said, finger tapping rapidly on the steering wheel. "First—this is really Pereira's find, but it'll be in my report, too—I yanked out a six-inch copper nail."

"From the base of the eucalypt?" I asked.

His finger stopped, arched back stiffly from the wheel. "One of four. I left the other three."

"And copper nails kill trees?"

"So people believe. I'll get the specifics, of course."

"*Four* nails," I said, feeling increasingly uneasy. "Someone is taking no chances. Or is even more obsessive than I'd thought. What's the second thing?"

Raksen shifted the gearstick into neutral, and began tapping his finger, more tentatively now. "I don't have test results yet, so this is off the record . . ." He waited till I nodded. "But Smith, someone has been pulling on your eucalyptus branch. They must have tossed a rope around the branch while the bark was still on it. Could be that the rope is what loosened the bark."

"What kind of rope?"

"No way to say. The bark is gone. Maybe there's a fiber I missed. I'm going to go over it again. But I doubt it."

If Raksen missed it, it didn't exist. "Thanks," I said.

I got in my VW, drove slowly out of the lot, and headed across Martin Luther King, Jr. Way, still thinking about Leila Sandoval. If she was hiding out, at least she wouldn't be at her house, near enough to Diamond's to cause any more harm. *She* wouldn't know that Kris had canceled the bees. Tonight, and as things now looked, tomorrow, she would be sitting smugly in whatever bolt-hole she'd chosen, expecting the bees to do her work. I stopped at the light on University Avenue. A gray-haired woman on a ten-speed slid in front of me. A man in a sports jacket, another in a suit, and one in an Indian dhoti crossed the street. It was already rush hour; I could be here for a while. I should have thought of that, have taken another route . . .

An obsessive person would have thought ahead. An obsessive wouldn't have trusted that the bees would arrive. She would have checked, found they'd been canceled. She'd be furious, and she would . . . do what?

The light changed. I inched closer to the intersection, wishing now that I had gotten to Kris before he canceled the bees. At least with them, we knew what to expect. Now I had no idea at all.

And there was nothing I could do but worry. What I needed was an hour swimming laps in the pool. Strong pulls, hard kicks. Real hard kicks. If I gave Mr. Kepple a brisk warning not to waste water (at least in sight of his neighbors), I just might make lap-swim hour.

It was a few minutes after five when I pulled up in front of Mr. Kepple's house, a standard green stucco in a middle-class neighborhood in north Berkeley. Two years ago I had rented the ten-by-forty back porch with its jalousie windows that held out neither rain nor the roar of Mr. Kepple's electric hedge trimmer, electric mower, blower, and seed sower, with indoor-outdoor carpet that resembled a golf course in monsoon season. I'd moved in because it was there and I was going through a divorce and any place was better than the house that held my ex-husband. Another impulsively grabbed pleasure, or lesser evil.

But it wasn't my inadequacies I was here to deal with. It was Mr. Kepple's. And I was certainly in the mood to point out someone else's faults.

I have interrogated hundreds of suspects. I've learned to read a suspect and play him like a fisherman, giving line, reeling in, letting out more and floating the slack on the water, then popping the button on the reel and cranking like mad. I've comforted victims too terrified to talk and eased them into giving statements. I've faced down guys who've spent more years in "Q" than out. But all that skill was useless when it came to talking to Mr. Kepple. When I lived in his converted back porch, my door opened onto the yard where he could be found digging or cutting, planting or yanking out any time of night or day. He had caught me racing out the door to work at seven A.M. (as he was spreading enough manure to become a major player in the state solid-waste disposal game). He'd been delighted to find company when I dragged home after a stakeout at four A.M. (when he was dispersing earthworms into the soil so they could find cover before the early birds indulged). There was no time of day or night when I was safe. He had devoured hours of my time describing his ever changing garden plans, pointing at the brown malodorous ground where the native plant section would be, at prospective Hollyhock Haven, at the site for the dry creek and wooden bridge in the upcoming Japanese garden. He had dragged out series after series of plot sketches he'd made in gardening class. (He'd even displayed several group pictures of his fellow gardening-class students—framed!) Lovingly, he'd shown me flats of baby plants that I knew would be discarded after a week in the ground, by which time he would have been seduced by a grander, or more colorful, or more subtle, more exotic, more natural, more seasonal, more *different* plan. He had—thank God—scorned plastic flamingos and terra cotta dwarfs. But there had been a tense week when he had realized he could get a good price on five giant Buddhas with differing hand positions. I had pictured the terra cotta statues sinking into the mud outside my door, leaving five bubbles of bad karma.

But even though nothing ever grew, Mr. Kepple had kept the soil ready. He'd added fertilizer weekly. And he never stopped watering.

That last proclivity of his was the problem. He was not responding responsibly to the drought. The neighbors had called the police. Again.

And, following the unwritten rule of professional courtesy, Murakawa had called me. Again.

With all that, I couldn't help but feel a fondness for the man. (Maybe it was guilt at my own parents being on the other side of the country, too far away to ask for my help.) And although I knew it wasn't remotely true, he had gotten to me every time he said, "The garden is for you, Jill. I want to see you walk out your door into the prettiest yard in Berkeley." With each new garden implement he was like a toddler tearing open his gifts on Christmas Eve. The time he got his leaf blower, he couldn't wait till morning to try it. (Actually, that hadn't seemed quite so endearing at the time. To me, or to the neighbors.)

The chances of convincing Mr. Kepple to withhold the water of life from his beloved garden were akin to convincing Hasbrouck Diamond to shade his nether parts from the sun.

But if there was ever a time I was prepared to stomp through his wall of intransigence, it was now.

No sound came from inside Mr. Kepple's pale green house. That didn't surprise me. I hadn't expected to find him in there when hours of sun were left. I made my way around the side. The path between his house and the hedge (blessedly, not one of those hedges that could be shaped like a lion or a cupid) was slate today. When I moved in it had been cement, then redwood slab, then wood chip, then a particularly slippery variety of ground cover.

The backyard was as I might have expected. Clusters of tiny green plants I couldn't name dotted the yard. Over the years they had all looked the same: small, green, flowerless, doomed. Despite the heat and drought, the grass was thick and vibrant green. But Mr. Kepple was nowhere in sight. And there was no roar, buzz, or spray.

"Mr. Kepple!" I called for form's sake. In the silence here, I didn't expect an answer. And I got none.

I opened the door to my old digs and got my second surprise. I had assumed that as soon as my last box was gone, Mr. Kepple would fill the porch with the equipment that had jammed his garage. Word was that he had for a while. But now, the ten-by-forty space looked like I still lived there. The chaise lounge was still at one end, the white wicker table and chairs in the middle, the bookcase at the near end by the spot where my sleeping bag had lain for those two years.

The flat was just waiting for me to move back in! I looked back at the ten-by-forty space, at the stained carpet, the one tiny closet, the walk-through kitchen that led to a bathroom so small that the toilet was set at an angle, with the edge of the sink extending over it, and the door had to be left open when I'd showered. My stomach clutched. I couldn't live here. After two months in The Palace, this place looked like . . . like a utility porch. On the other hand, if I didn't find an apartment this weekend . . . "Mr. Kepple!"

In the next yard, beyond the hedge, a door opened. Mr. Kepple's neighbor, a woman a few years older than I—maybe thirty-five—stalked out onto a porch about level with my head. A T-shirt clung clammily to her chest, thin blond hair hung limp and stringy, and on her pale, sweaty face was a scowl. She stared down at my green shirt and gray slacks and my businesslike loop earrings.

"Are you from the water department?" she demanded. She didn't recognize me. That was a relief. But then, when I lived here I had had little chance to be out in the yard to be seen.

I walked toward her. The overhanging hedge would block her view of all but the top of my head. "No. I'm a friend. I need to talk to Mr. Kepple."

"Damn right!" she snapped. "*Somebody* needs to talk to the man. Look at that yard! It's a swamp! Do you know how many times the man watered yesterday? Six times. In one day! The man's got no sense!"

The anger I'd been swallowing all day pushed to the surface. Not that I doubted the truth of her complaint. But the plants under the hedge were limp. He hadn't watered six times today. Still, I could hear the sharp edge to my voice when I said, "I'll have a talk—"

"We've got to save water. I've told him. But does he listen?"

I knew the answer to that. I inched closer to the hedge. Standing in the shade, I looked down at the drooping plants. Mr. Kepple was every bit as obsessive as Leila Sandoval or Hasbrouck Diamond. He would never let his plants droop.

"I told him," the woman told me, her face growing pink, "we *all* have to conserve. I heat dishwater on the stove so I don't have to run the water till it gets hot. We empty the rinse water in the garden. We don't shower anymore; we just soap and rinse off. The kids get a prize each week for shortest time in the shower. We're killing ourselves saving water. But whatever we save, *he* wastes."

What I needed to do was keep my mouth shut, leave a note for Mr. Kepple, and get out of here. Howard would be at the pool, standing at the shallow end, waiting for me, the sunlight glistening off his curly red hair, water dripping down his chest, tracing the line of his pectoral muscles.

"Did Kepple ever listen?" she yelled, shaking her head. "The man's impossible."

I looked back at the wilted plants. How long had it taken them to sag like this? An hour? Four hours? All day? Mr. Kepple the obsessive . . . I remembered Howard at the pool Tuesday, flicking a drop of water off my arm, letting his hand rest there.

Howard had said, "We could skip lap swim tonight. We swam yesterday." "There's a bottle of Zinfandel in the fridge," I'd said. The same verbal foreplay we could be having in a few minutes. I could almost feel his fingers quivering against my skin, or was it the other way around? I stared down at the wilting plants. Despite the heat a shiver ran down my back. Picturing the pool and Howard pushing off, gliding underwater, without me, I sighed. To the neighbor, I said, "Has Mr. Kepple been watering today?"

She pounded her fist on her porch railing. "Selfish old bastard! Doesn't care about anyone but himself!"

Be calm, I told myself. But I was already stepping out from the protection of the hedge. "Mr. Kepple doesn't *have* anyone but himself. His wife is dead. All he has is his yard. Maybe you'd like to practice showing compassion during all those minutes you, and your husband, and your children save by not showering. Maybe you could earn a prize, too."

She stared, open-mouthed. Before she could regroup, I said, "Now tell me, when was the last time you saw him out here watering?"

"Last night, but—"

"Last night? Today's the hottest day of the year. Where has he been today?"

"Not here, thank God . . ." But some of the anger had drained from her voice. "I don't know where he is."

I ran around to the front and pounded on the door. No sound came from inside. There was no green glow from the television (Mr. Kepple's idea of burglar-proofing). I ran downstairs and peered into the garage. His pickup truck was inside.

I grabbed the front door key from under the rock by the stairs and ran back up the stairs. Unlocking the door I walked in, calling his name.

He wasn't there. I picked up his phone and dialed the dispatcher at the station and asked him to check his records. If Mr. Kepple had had an accident in Berkeley, if an ambulance had been called in an emergency, it would be on the dispatcher's log.

I sat waiting, looking around the living room. The sofa was a brown tweed, frayed, the carpet green, worn. Everything needed dusting. In front of the television a Naugahyde recliner stood, its footrest still up. There were three rips in the plastic, two taped over with gray tape. A beer can lay on the floor next to it. Although I had never been in the room long enough to survey it like this, none of what I saw surprised me. Until I looked at the mantel. It was crowded with photos. In the center was a gold framed wedding picture of the Kepples that must have been forty years old. In it was a young Mr. Kepple, his hair too brown, his cheeks too pink in the photographic tint.

He looked not nervous or stiff, but downright cocky. And Mrs. Kepple, who had died before I moved in, had a shy but knowing smile. Through the unnatural tint of the picture, she looked not pretty exactly, but warm, friendly, and yet . . . What exactly did that picture purvey? Wry. She looked wry. It was not the first characteristic I would have expected of a wife of Mr. Kepple. There were seven photos, taken, I guessed, every fifth anniversary. The Kepples smiled at each other in every one, the cockiness of his grin fading with each interval, her knowing smile softening to one of compassion. In the last one, maybe seven years old now, the two expressions had been nearly the same.

But it wasn't the expression itself that surprised me. What surprised me was the look of understanding, one I had never seen on Mr. Kepple's face.

What was taking the dispatcher so long?

I glanced at the wall behind the recliner, at group photos from Mr. Kepple's classes. WEEDS said the sign in front of the dozen or so students in the top one. PESTS was in the middle. And at the bottom TREES. I looked closer at TREES. Mr. Kepple was at the far right of the eight students. At the left, standing a bit away from the other seven was the blond boy with the tattoo of the cypress on his back and shoulders, the boy who had been talking to Leila Sandoval and Herman Ott this afternoon.

"Smith?" the dispatcher said. "The call came early this morning, a nine eleven call to Alta Bates Hospital."

MR. KEPPLE had fallen and broken his leg. That was the good news. The bad news was that they didn't know why. Tomorrow they would run tests. It might have been a stroke.

I walked slowly down the beige hospital hall to his room. I hadn't pictured what he'd look like, but when I stepped into Mr. Kepple's room he looked worse than I was prepared for. Mr. Kepple, who I was used to seeing bent over a wheelbarrow or hoisting a burlap-bound sapling, lay in the bed, gray, small, and rubbery looking. His eyes weren't quite closed. Carefully, I put a hand on his arm and whispered, "Mr. Kepple?"

He didn't move.

I hesitated to say his name louder, in case he really was asleep. I pulled up a chair next to his bed and watched him breathe. And tried not to imagine what life would be for him if he couldn't move one side of his body, if he could never bend down and plant a six-pack of violets, or yank out a rhododendron.

Suddenly Hasbrouck Diamond and Leila Sandoval seemed less than childish squabblers. They were fools to

71

toss away precious hours or whole days or weeks fuming at each other. Hasbrouck Diamond was an idiot to sit stubbornly under a branch that could fall and maim him. And Leila Sandoval, what variety of villain was she to take even the chance of killing Bev Zagoya to nourish her petty revenge? And Herman Ott? Had he been party to Sandoval's disappearance or had she merely made use of him? Herman Ott's own unavailability could mean any of a number of things. And the boy with the cypress tattoo, who had been talking first to Leila and then to Ott, just where did he fit in? Was he a courier carrying her desperate plea to a responsive Ott? Or just a kid who happened by and spoke to two acquaintances? And who was he, anyway? How consistent with my day that I had before me the one person who knew the boy's real name, and he couldn't speak to me.

I looked down at Mr. Kepple and felt a wave of guilt about that last thought. But, I reminded myself, Mr. Kepple of all people would understand self-absorption.

The bed next to him was empty. The room was dark now, lit only by a dim fixture over the bed, one of those dull lights that seem to suck the illumination into it rather than spreading it out. Two feet from the bed, I couldn't have seen to read. But reading didn't occur to me. The room had taken on a reality of its own, pulling me into the rhythm of Mr. Kepple's breathing. The regularity of the sound was lulling and I found myself sinking back in the chair, wedging my feet against the bedside table. Every so often, his breath would catch, he'd give a high wheeze, and I would jerk forward, pierced by fear of what his diagnosis might be, fear intensified by the sight of his pale, pale face. Then the shortness of his breaths reminded me of the terror that might lie beneath his eyelids. Or maybe nothing lay there.

I should have gone on home. It was foolish to stay. But I couldn't bare to have him wake up in a strange place with no one around. I kept thinking of those pictures on his mantel, and of Mrs. Kepple who wasn't here for him. I wondered if he had sat in a hospital like this watching her breathe, and cease to breathe.

I wondered if there would be a time, thirty, forty years from now, when I would sit in a chair like this and watch Howard cease to breathe. Or, considering his line of work, a time sooner. I couldn't bring myself to picture Howard's face gray like Mr. Kepple's or his eyes empty. I knew I couldn't allow myself to think of it at all. There are times for gallows humor in police work; it protects us. There are times when the unspoken law of police etiquette forbids it: we don't laugh about death when the dead are kids or old people, or other cops. Then all our fury goes into getting the bastards who did it. But in a way the two reactions are the same thing. Both protect us; both allow us to keep going and do the job we're paid for. And yet every time we hone this skill we push the realization of death deeper down farther from consideration, and the unfaced fear gains strength in the darkness.

I stood up and went in search of a phone to call Howard. But when I dialed, I got no answer at my place and the machine at his. I called the dispatcher—no word from patrol—then dialed information and got Sandoval's number and dialed her. No answer. Then, for form's sake, I tried Ott. I could picture him perching next to the phone, yellow bathrobe over yellow nightshirt (I'd woken him up often enough over the years to know his nocturnal garb) and a smug look on his sallow face as he listened to me talk to his machine.

I walked back to Mr. Kepple's room and sat for half an hour, a draft moving across my shoulders, medicinal odors I couldn't name tainting the air. Uncomfortable as the chair was I dozed.

Mr. Kepple woke up around two A.M. He looked right at me.

"Mr. Kepple," I said.

73

"Flo?" he asked.

Flo? Mrs. Kepple? "No, it's me, Jill. Jill Smith?"

"Oh." His eyes misted. It was a full minute before he said, "Not Flo." Then his eyes closed again.

I swallowed, wondering if she lived each night in his dreams, or if I was making that up.

Mr. Kepple woke twice more. The second time I told him who I was and he repeated my name, but I couldn't tell whether he knew what that word meant. I didn't know whether my sitting in the chair all night had made the slightest difference to him, if he even realized I was there or remembered it once his eyes closed.

At four fifteen, a nurse woke me up.

"Are you Detective Smith?" she asked.

I nodded.

She handed me a piece of paper. "Call this number."

Back cramped, neck tight, one hand numb from falling asleep on that side, I stood up.

Mr. Kepple groaned. His eyes opened. He stared straight ahead, eyes fixed with the look of terror I had hoped he'd be spared. "Hospital?" he asked.

"It's okay, Mr. Kepple."

"What am I doing here?"

I rang to get the nurse back. "You had a fall. You broke your leg. You'll be okay now."

"What time is it?"

"Four twenty."

"Twenty after four!" His grayish face looked even paler. "After four! I needed to get the sprinkler on at three. Before they come home from work."

I didn't have to say who "they" were. I caught myself before I could say it was four in the *morning*. "Don't worry, Mr. Kepple, I checked the plants, they're fine."

"Sprinkler . . . dahlia . . . salpiglossis."

I gave his hand a squeezed and smiled. "The plants will be fine, Mr. Kepple."

74

He nodded. His skin looked as if it had loosened. It reacted to the movement of his chin an instant late. "Jill?"

"Yes?" I bent closer.

"You'll take care of them, won't you? You can turn the sprinkler on when you go out to work."

He'd forgotten I didn't live there anymore. "Yes," I said, knowing there was no other answer, "of course I'll take care of the garden."

"You're a nice girl, Jill." He sighed. His face relaxed. In a moment he was asleep again. He hadn't asked about his own condition.

Shaking my head, I hurried out to the phone and dialed the number on the paper: the dispatcher.

"Berkeley Police Department."

"Five twenty-seven," I said.

"Ah, Smith." He paused a moment, to check his log, I knew. But I wouldn't have had to wait for him to give me the particulars. The dispatcher's tone is always the first clue. I recognized that mixture of adrenaline, regret, and curiosity. I knew it would be a 187 (homicide) before he told me. But I didn't guess that the address would be Dr. Hasbrouck Diamond's.

It took me less than twenty minutes to drive to the base of Panoramic Way.

Overnight the fog had blown in, thick, gray, cold. Pulser lights from patrol cars and the spinner atop the ambulance flashed off the retaining wall across the street, off the fog-wet NO PARKING ANY TIME sign, off the pavement, off the finish of the other cars. There was light in every window in every house. Thick morning fog fuzzed the yellow light in the windows, and the street looked like an Advent calendar on Christmas Day. Lights on second floors went out; lights downstairs came on. The patrol cars blocked driveways (the street was too narrow to double-park in). The squeals from the radios filtered into the fog. Farther up the street I spotted Raksen's van. A couple of civilian cars I recognized as belonging to newspeople stuck out at odd angles at the switchback. I pulled in front of another driveway and hurried down to Diamond's house, shivering in the shirt that had been too heavy yesterday.

A surprisingly large crowd peered over the hedge and pressed at the yellow plastic "rope" the scene supervisor had put up. About half of them looked like reporters; two had cameras.

"Detective Smith," one of them called.

"I just got here," I said, stepping over the barricade and making my way onto the deck.

The lights from Hasbrouck Diamond's living room came through the big glass doors. In the post-dawn fog they had the same depressing after-the-party look as dirty glasses and overflowing ashtrays abandoned on tables and chair arms. Inside, I could see the poster-size photos of huge icy mountains, of Nepali villages at the foot of them, of Bev Zagoya at the peak of one, planting a flag. I saw geometric quilts in red and blue and black prints, and a cloth wall hanging depicting Tibetan demons that hadn't been there yesterday. The room was set up for Bev Zagoya's presentation. Vaguely I wondered who would call all the invitees and cancel.

I looked at the spot where Hasbrouck Diamond had been sitting when the eucalyptus branch fell. It wouldn't have surprised me to find his corpse right there. But nothing was there, neither Hasbrouck Diamond, nor his chair.

I walked toward the end of the deck where Hasbrouck Diamond's rappelling wall went forty feet down. The gate was open.

Martinez, the crime scene supervisor, put up a hand. "Watch it!"

"Watch what?"

Martinez pointed to the deck floor.

76

I had to bend closer to see what he was protecting. Hunkered down I could make out the two long skid marks. They led off the edge of the deck.

"Down there," Martinez said as I stood up. "The chaise lounge went over the end. He went headfirst. Landed on his head. Snapped his neck."

I moved around him to the edge of the deck. There's an odd silence that comes at that moment when you know you're going to see the body, a body that used to be a person you knew. It's as if a bubble surrounds you, blocking the patrol car squeals, the murmuring of the crowd, the slap of shoe leather against the redwood decking, and what you hear is your own breathing, and the eucalyptus leaves rustling in the cold, fog-laden wind.

Careful to avoid the skid marks, I looked down into the brush and poison oak, and the light that surrounded the body.

I hadn't actually formed the thought, but I had assumed the victim would be Hasbrouck Diamond. I was prepared for that. I hadn't liked Diamond, and that would have made it a little easier.

But I had liked Kris Mouskavachi. And I didn't want him to be dead. And Kris Mouskavachi was certainly dead.

10

THE only way to get to the spot where Kris lay, other than the route he himself had taken, was to go back through the deck arch, down the sidewalk, around the switchback to the yard below Diamond's, up the path, over the yellow plastic "rope," and twenty feet up the steep, rocky brush- and poison-oak-covered incline.

I took a breath as I neared the body, but it didn't help. After the last ceremony when new officers were sworn, I had taken a couple of the women aside and said, "Berkeley's a small town. There are going to be times when you roll out and find the corpse of a friend's mother, or child, or the friend himself. You're going to feel like shit. But no matter how bad you feel, how justified that is, remember this: Women cops don't cry. A guy cries, people think that's a sign he's human, but if a tear rolls down a woman officer's cheek, she loses credibility forever."

I stared into fog-dark underbrush and listened to one of the patrol guys up on the deck, talking to Martinez, talking about the DOA, about Kris. "Helluva way to get up in the morning, huh?"

"Yeah." It was Martinez. "Regular Cannonball Run."

"Berkeley Airlines Supersaver!" They both laughed. I would have laughed had I not known Kris. But even having known him, the gallows humor was working. I felt that therapeutic distance forming. And I looked down not quite so much at the boy who'd made me an iced cappuccino, but more at "the deceased."

The chaise lounge had landed right side up, the end wedged against a tree. Kris's head had hit a slab of rock and the force of the flight had flipped his body over, so now he lay with his legs, pelvis, and lower ribs across the chaise, the back of his head still on the rock. It didn't take any esoteric knowledge to see that his neck had snapped. His nose—not his chin, but his *nose*—was pressed into his breastbone.

Surely, I thought, he couldn't have lived long after the impact, probably only seconds. But he'd bled a lot. Head wounds do. Brown, dried blood coated his hair and the rock, like wax that has dripped from a fast-burning candle. I wondered how Raksen would deal with that when he moved the body. Would the blood pull at Kris's hair?

I turned away and swallowed hard, and came within a breath of losing my credibility.

Kris's right hand clutched the metal arm of the lounge. That watch of his with the map of Switzerland was still running. The gallows thought crossed my mind: an advertisement for Swiss watches. "You may crash to your death, but your Swiss watch will keep ticking."

I took Raksen's flashlight, bent down, and looked more closely at that watch. The case was gold, as was the map of Switzerland and the lettering of the German name beneath it, one I'd never heard of. It was an expensive-looking watch for a boy like Kris to have. To Raksen, I said, "I'll need this watch when you're done."

Raksen nodded. "Couldn't budge the fingers. He must have been asleep when the chaise went. Must have woken up, half awake, grabbed." Raksen shrugged.

"Didn't help. Might even be what broke his neck. He must of slipped off when the cushion went, hit his head, and then got caught on the chaise."

I shivered, suddenly aware of the icy fog. It had soaked into my light shirt. The fabric lay cold, clammy against my back, and somehow that made me feel Kris's death all the more.

"I can't say for sure," Raksen went on. "I'm just finishing the first roll of film. I'll need to check the trajectories for the chaise and for him and the cushion, too. The runners on the chaise have oil on them."

I shook my head ruefully. "The chaise up there just waiting for someone to oil its runner; the gate ready to be opened: it's like the whole deck was planned to kill Kris."

"There are no slide marks down here, Smith. The chaise, and the body, hit and struck."

"Ambulance?" I asked, for form's sake. If there's the remotest chance of resuscitation we roll the ambulance.

Raksen shook his head. "No question. When I got here half of his head was purple. What I could see of his face was waxy yellow, and his eyes were already dull."

I bent down again and balanced mostly on my downhill foot to get a view of Kris's face. Raksen was right. The fluid in the eyes had already dried out. I felt his chin; it was cold, as I'd expected, but despite the jammed position, still pliable. I slipped my hand under Kris's shirt. His chest was warmer, but not a whole lot.

"He slept outside, on the chaise, Smith."

"Wonderful!" I snapped. "So much for the ever unreliable body temp."

"Blanket's over there."

I flashed the light on Kris's hand. He was clutching nothing but the metal chair arm. I stood up. "You done photographing?"

"I've only taken one roll, all of the body. I still need angles, and ground. I'd like to wait for more light."

"No chance. You can't leave the body lying here on display. Martinez will have enough trouble keeping the scene secure with all those reporters out there. Get what you need now to place the body and call the coroner. You can do the ground and the footprints—"

"What there are on this surface," Raksen said, staring down at the dry rocky underbrush.

"Do that later. For now, finish with him, then let's do his pockets."

I stepped back, retracing my steps, and watched as Raksen wedged a foot against a tree trunk and aimed his Mamiya.

A four-foot-wide stripe of ground turned red, then dark, then red again; tires squealed as the patrol car took the switchback corner. Above, I could hear feet hitting the deck, Martinez's voice, Pereira's voice. And then one I didn't recognize said, "What's this gate?" He had to be eyeing the deck gate through which Kris had fallen. *Last Exit to Brooklyn?* Martinez said with a laugh. More footsteps tapped on the deck. Guys on beat, off-duty officers, anyone who was awake when the squeal came over the radio, or who had a friend willing to wake him, would be rolling to the scene. A 187 is always a draw, but a homicide at the well-known address of the well-known Has-Bitched Diamond would be a circus. Martinez would spend half his time just keeping the sworn officers off the evidence.

Making a wide circle, Raksen moved to the far side of the body and refocused his camera.

How many Himalayan expeditions had Kris Mouska-vachi been on? Even if the number was no more than one, that meant he had chanced avalanches, blizzards, rotten rock, hidden crevasses, hazards that kill one out of ten experienced climbers. And then died falling off a Berkeley deck.

I recalled the skid marks Martinez had pointed out. Being *pushed* off a Berkeley deck.

It was another twenty minutes and several prods from me before Raksen conceded, grudgingly, that he might have enough exposures. There had been a bet once, when Raksen was handling the scene of a drug-related killing, just how long Raksen would continue to photograph the body and the scene if no one stopped him. Howard, of course, had been the creator of that contest. No one won. No one had that much patience.

Covering his hand with a plastic bag, Raksen extricated the wallet from Kris's back pocket. It was new, leather, and held nothing but a one-dollar bill, a twenty, and a folded piece of paper with an address in Humboldt County. I copied the address.

Now Raksen called the nearest patrol officer. She lifted the body and stretched it out on its back while Raksen supported the neck so there was no question of "undertaker's fracture" there. The hair was still glued to the stone.

Placing a plastic bag over his head Raksen reached in the left jean pocket.

"Empty."

The right one held change and two keys. Nothing worth the wait. I walked back the way I'd come to the deck. Martinez was talking to Pereira. A lazy or hostile crime scene supervisor can triple your work. Witnesses can leave the scene before he assigns someone to get their statements or even their names. He can leave unroped the alley through which the "responsible" ran. He can allow samples to go unlabeled, or mislabeled. He can destroy an investigation entirely. Conversely, a good crime supe. is a pearl of great price. And Martinez was the biggest pearl around. Martinez made it his business to know each of us in D.D., in what order we worked, with whom we worked best. I suspected it was he who had called Pereira, and might call Murakawa. And I wasn't surprised when he said, "Leonard and Acosta are on the neighbors, except Sandoval. I sent Pereira there."

"She's gone," Pereira grumbled.

"Did it look like she just left or that she hadn't been home all night?"

Pereira shrugged. "Nothing to suggest she's been here. But she could have been."

Martinez said, "Diamond's in the living room with Murakawa. Has been for half an hour. Murakawa looks done with him. Zagoya's upstairs with Heling. No one else in the house."

"Neighbors see anything? Or *hear* anything?"

"Not so far, and Leonard got the neighbors one house down. No scream. That's what you're asking, right, Smith?"

"Right."

"No scream."

"What about the crash? Even if the boy didn't scream the chaise lounge had to have made a thud when it landed."

Pereira shook her head. "Neighbors here, Smith, are used to tuning out the goings-on at Diamond's. It'd take a lot more than a thud in the middle of the night to light a fire under them."

Martinez's eyes narrowed, but he censored whatever rebuke he'd considered. To me he said, "Diamond's asking for you."

I motioned Pereira to relieve Murakawa. "And when we're done," I said to her, "let's go over your financial check on Diamond, Bev Zagoya, and Sandoval. Let's see what it takes to run a house on Panoramic Way."

"Damn sight more then foot massage," Pereira muttered. She walked into the living room and took Murakawa's place.

Murakawa had once planned to be a chiropractor. He

83

emerged from the living room, glanced back at Diamond, and shook his head. "Worse kyphosis I've seen on a living being, his age. How could he do that to himself? Doesn't the guy ever look in the mirror?" He paused. "Well, I guess not." Now he looked back at the slumping Diamond and sighed. "I'd give a week's wages to see X-rays of his thoracic and cervical vertebrae. Head slumped like that. He must have no disk space at all at his anterior vertebrae, must be bone on bone."

"His statement, Murakawa?"

Murakawa handed me his notes. "You know, Smith, I don't even think surgery could restore the normal curves to that spine, and I wouldn't think about surgery unless . . ." He shook his head again. "Maybe a treatment of muscle relaxers, massage, and weekly adjustments . . ."

Ignoring Murakawa's ongoing diagnosis, I read over his notes on Diamond's statement. Diamond had ordered dinner from Thyme-wise, the gourmet takeout shop on Solano. He and Bev Zagoya had spent the three hours from seven to ten in the living room going over plans for their presentations in the morning. Kris was still out when he went to bed. If that was true, whoever oiled the runners of the chaise had to have done so before seven or after ten. *If* Diamond's statement was true.

I took a last look down at Kris Mouskavachi's body, then headed back though the yard below, around the switchback to the sidewalk, and onto the deck. The darkness had thinned to a cold gray. Fog draped from the tops of live oaks to the branches of the eucalypts. And the icy wind off the Bay flapped those carp flags at the corners of Diamond's roof and ripped loose shreds of fog and carried them away.

The light in the living room came from spots in the ceiling and over the posters. White on white. Yesterday in the heat this large white room had seemed comfortable, but today it was just cold, and the thick carpet made it not warmer but merely more irritating to walk across. I glanced at Himalayan-size photographs of Himalaya. The most interesting one had to have been taken from a mountain top, down onto ice, then the brown of dirt and the ever darkening green of fields and the tan of a village. There was an arrogance to that photograph, and as I looked at it I could almost imagine the heady thrill of standing where few if any men had ever trod, looking down on the world of lesser beings.

Slumped on the edge of a huge white sectional, Hasbrouck Diamond was the picture of a lesser being. He sat slumped forward, staring down. The thick gold chain around his neck swayed back and forth in midair. The shine of his royal blue silk shirt only made his tanned face look drier, and white shorts showed shivering spindly beige thighs. He looked like he'd spent too much time with the movie types in L.A., immersed in the unreal. And yet there was no question that the man was seriously shaken.

Sitting beside him I said, "Dr. Diamond, what can you tell me about yesterday?" When he didn't respond I prompted, "After you talked to me?"

"I was here, all day, except for a trip to the hardware store. The bulb on the projector was out. We need that for the presentation, it's this afternoon, you know." He swallowed. "Or it would have been. I have to call all those people. Some of them are flying up from L.A. I have to get to them before they leave for the airport. Can't have them flying up here and find nothing. I'll have to—"

"Dr. Diamond," I snapped.

"Oh." He gave his head a sharp shake, and looked up at me. "Sorry." The dark circles under his eyes gave the illusion that they protruded more than they did normally, almost as if they were feelers. He appeared more foreign and yet because of his drained, bewildered look, more human than he had seemed yesterday. "Yesterday," he repeated. "I was here, taking calls, going over the figures. I was here all day. I guess I could come up with a list of who I spoke to if you need it."

"Figures?"

He looked up, brow furrowed. I tried to categorize his expression—fear, sorrow, confusion? None of those. "We had to plan, Detective. You don't invite two hundred of the most influential people in the Bay Area, expect them to become a part of a history-making Himalayan expedition, and not have your figures straight."

"Figures for?" I insisted.

"For everything, gear for the climbing team, the filming team, and the Sherpas, and the porters, food, air fare, arrangements for the receptions after the climb. It's all detail work. We need to be able to tell them how many pounds of *tsampa* Bev'll buy and how many anoraks the team will need."

"And you discussed that with Bev? When did she get back?" I had seen her at Indian Rock around three P.M.

"Seven or so. We worked till ten." Self-absorbed as Hasbrouck Diamond was, he was proving to be remarkably easy to prod. His glance upward had been brief; now he was directing his answers to his knees. He probably was barely aware I was next to him.

"Where was Kris?"

"Kris?" Diamond's pale eyebrows drew together and he began to tap his forefinger on his thigh. "Who knows? Hanging around on the Avenue, probably. He should have been here. I had expected him to help out with the planning; told him when he got back."

"And that was?"

"Somewhere around eleven. I was getting ready for bed. I suggested that he do that too. We needed to be fresh this morn— Or I thought we would."

"How did Kris seem then, last night?"

Diamond hesitated; his face colored and that finger tapped more heavily on his thigh, leaving a paler circle in its aftermath. "Like he always was, happy-go-lucky."

I wondered if happy-go-lucky was really what he'd thought of Kris Mouskavachi, the charming Kathmandu wheeler-dealer. "What did you talk about with Kris?"

"Nothing. I was going to bed. He clearly wasn't."

"Do you know what time he did go to bed?"

All four fingers now tapped. "How would I? My bedroom's upstairs. I wouldn't hear him walk out onto the deck."

"So he slept on the deck," I prompted.

"Always," he snapped. "He always slept on the deck."

"Why?"

"He liked it. I gave him a room upstairs. My best guest room. He said it was bigger than his family's living room. He said he loved it. But he never slept up there. He said he liked sleeping outside. Said it reminded him of being on an expedition." His fingers knotted into a fist.

"Dr. Diamond, had Kris gotten any threatening calls, or even any odd calls? Did he have any friends who might have—"

He slammed his fist into his thigh and glared directly at me. "Why do you waste your time asking about Kris? It's me she tried to kill!"

11

I DIDN'T have to ask who the "she" was Diamond was accusing of trying to murder him.

I did ask, of course. According to him, Leila Sandoval must have seen a figure sleeping under a blanket on the chaise lounge, the very chaise on which Diamond habitually sat. Naturally assuming the body was his, she had opened the gate and given the chaise a shove. Diamond said that he was in the habit of keeping a blanket next to him on the chaise lounge, in case the sun went in. He could get cold, he had reminded me. And recalling his epidermal state when sunbathing, I couldn't help but agree.

There were nights, after parties, he went on, when he had fallen asleep out there. Recalling Pereira's description of those parties (the social equivalent of Mr. Kepple's mower, blower, and electric seed sower?) and the neighbors' complaints, I could imagine Diamond falling asleep, or more likely passing out on the chaise. According to him, he had only ceased sleeping there when Kris took over the spot. And that, he added, was not something Leila Sandoval was likely to notice, particularly since, as even *I* must have realized, Sandoval hadn't been home much lately. He had actually raised his head to watch my reaction when he added that Leila Sandoval wouldn't have minded if she had failed to kill him, as long as she managed to make him a laughing stock and ruin Bev Zagoya's reception this morning. "Which she did!" he had concluded with a grisly sort of triumph.

I sat a moment looking across the thick carpet, then said, "Let me see Kris's room."

Diamond pushed himself up, a slow awkward movement more suited to his posture than his age or his interests. He shuffled across the carpet and up the stairs to the second floor. The staircase bisected the house and, I noted, continued on up to the roof. To the west of it was one large room—Diamond's, he indicated—with windows from which on a fogless day he might have seen the Golden Gate Bridge and the Farallon Islands beyond. The east half was divided unevenly into two rooms, and the bedroom he indicated as Kris's was nearly twice the size of the other. Like everything else it was white, with a white quilted double bed, and white lacquered desk, chair, and dresser. Two Himalayan posters decorated one wall, and an antique-looking Tibetan Thangka, a vividly colored cloth depiction of the Tibetan deities, hung across from it. On a shelf was a large statue of the Hindu god Siva, dancing in a ring of fire. I checked the desk, dresser, and closet. The clothes there were basic: a spare pair of jeans and two shirts, a couple of changes of underwear. The adjoining bathroom held minimal supplies. It could have been a hotel room. A carefully decorated hotel room.

"There's nothing personal here," I said.

Diamond leaned against the doorjamb. It was a moment before he said, "He was on a budget."

And in that moment I could see the stab that my words had been. Nothing *personal*. Nothing in return for Hasbrouck Diamond's hospitality. He didn't move or make a sound, but all his anger and drive melted and he *became* no more than his slumped posture.

I looked again at the Thangka and the bronze Siva. The same friend who had told me about the pasture saying had shown me some of her Indian art. Unless I missed my guess, what Diamond had here was expensive. "Did you decorate the room for him?"

He nodded.

This expensively decorated room was the last type of place that would have appealed to a teenager, much less Kris Mouskavachi, the future CEO. Left to Kris this room would have sported posters of San Francisco with the Transamerica pyramid in the foreground and "Feinstein for Governor," a computer, a TV, a VCR, a Walkman, a CD player, Lee Iacocca's biography on the night table, and in the closet lots and lots of stylish clothes. But if he'd had to accept the room as is, my take on Kris was that living in here would have appealed to him a whole lot more than sleeping on the deck.

The windows in Kris's room faced away from the deck, an arrangement that would have given Diamond more privacy down there.

Or up here.

I looked around the room again. Was the emptiness in here merely an indication of Kris's lack of commitment to Hasbrouck Diamond, or was it a much more pointed rejection? Charming, eager-to-be-liked Kris would have been an easy boy to misjudge. "Dr. Diamond," I said, "what exactly was the relationship between you and Kris?"

Without looking up, he said, "Kris was my guest, my responsibility. I cared about the boy. Although he'd only been with me six weeks, it was kind of like having a son. I showed him Berkeley, I took him to my spot on Orchard Lane. I told him"—Diamond swallowed—"how it's like a three-minute vacation in Florence there. But he didn't understand. He didn't even know what Florence was like; he'd never been anywhere but Kathmandu and Delhi. Having Kris here was nice . . . comfortable . . . having him here. I like company. Bev was in the Alps when he arrived, so, you see, I had a chance to really know him, just like a son."

"Any sexual attraction?"

His eyes snapped open. "Hardly. Detective, I was responsible for the boy. And I, Detective, am not attracted to boys."

"What about Bev Zagoya? You were attracted to her."

His face softened. I recalled that look of pride he'd had the first time he mentioned her. "I am," he said, "very fond of Bev. Fond and very, very proud. You'd have to ask her if that feeling is mutual."

I nodded, noting the odd terms he had used, ones that would certainly not be mutual. "And Leila Sandoval? You were involved with her, weren't you?"

"That lunatic! Detective, haven't I made myself clear about her? I—"

"The truth, Dr. Diamond."

"I don't expect to be—"

"Enough!" I said, glaring down at him. "A boy's been murdered. You say that attack was meant for you. Maybe so. Now I don't have time for lies. I want to know exactly what went on between you and Sandoval, and how it relates to everything that's happened since."

For a moment he didn't move. Outside the branch of a live oak brushed against the window pane. Red lights from one of the pulsers flashed and then were gone. Diamond sank down on the corner of Kris's unused white bed. His head hung. He muttered, "She lived next door. It was just convenience. I thought for a while there was something in her, some drive, some flash of specialness, some small speck of what Bev is made of. But there wasn't. But it was convenient. I had my Thursdays off.

She was here. Her husband was at work. It was an amusement for a while. Just temporary. Just a convenience."

"But not for her?" I prodded, sitting beside him where I could get a better view of his face.

Diamond shrugged.

"She and her husband separated, didn't they?"

His jaw tightened. "That wasn't my fault. I didn't encourage that. Whatever great flourish of emotion that lunatic woman chose to indulge, I did not demand." He looked directly at me. "Detective, Lucas Sandoval was a sensible man. He was an engineer. He saw his chance to escape the lunatic, got himself transferred, and pressed for divorce. If you ask me he'd probably been looking for a way out for years. And considering what's happened to me, and now to Kris, Lucas Sandoval was damned smart."

Diamond slumped farther forward, the picture of depression. And self-protection. It's hard to talk to a man's back or side, or the top of his head. Suddenly, the sight of him, his incredible protective self-absorption, made me furious. And despite my feelings about Leila Sandoval I sympathized with her. Then Hasbrouck Diamond surprised me.

"Kris was my guest," he said. "My responsibility. I will call his parents and give them the news."

I hesitated momentarily, hating to remove the onus of that task from him. "That's not—"

"No. It is." His hands squeezed back into fists. Despite his tan, his face had taken on a jaundiced look. "Besides," he muttered, "I am a periodontist. I have a lot of experience in making bad news palatable." A weak smile flashed on his face. He blushed, swallowed, let his head hang back to its normal position, and said, "Sorry, a little dental humor there. Hardly the time for it."

"Dr. Diamond, that's a generous offer. But notification of survivors in a murder case is a police function.

When I call the Mouskavachis I will tell them that you intended to let them know." Looking at Diamond I wondered if his rare display of consideration was generated by a sorrow over Kris's death, a horror at the thought that Kris had died in his place, or just the hollow terror of thinking that it could have been himself on the way to the morgue. Or all three. Or perhaps there was something he didn't want the Mouskavachis telling me.

12

I LET Diamond go. He trudged into his own pristine room, looking like a troll who'd made a wrong turn and wandered into the Hall of the Elf Kings.

I went downstairs to the deck, motioned Martinez over, and told him to have Leonard go back to the neighbors who had a view of that chaise and find out who they would have expected to find on it. Acosta he sent up to the roof garden to relieve Heling, who had taken Zagoya's statement and was now babysitting the climber. When Heling came down I went over the statement with her. Zagoya's story matched Diamond's: They both said they had been working on their presentation. Kris had been out. They finished about ten. She went to bed about eleven.

Then I climbed the two flights to the roof. The roof garden was a redwood-floored rectangle with a redwood railing, redwood chairs and tables, and flower boxes filled with red geraniums. It would have made a much better sundeck than the deck below. Here Hasbrouck Diamond could have sat unshaded by eucalyptus, unendangered by threats from branches. This morning, like most mornings, it was still thick in fog. But if Bev Zagoya missed the sun, she gave no indication. Hose in hand, she was bending over one of the geranium-filled planters that lined the edges of the roof. Geraniums are not flowers you see much anymore, outside of posters of Switzerland (a thought which I would be careful *not* to pass on to Mr. Kepple). These made an odd mixture with the red Chinese turrets at the corners, and the fish socks that hung limply from them. Dissonant but not ineffective.

"Dissonant" summed up the impression I got looking at Bev Zagoya. In red silky running shorts and a bright yellow tank top, she seemed oblivious to the chill of the fog. I would not have credited her tense face and haphazard movements to sorrow, or anger, or even the shock of Kris Mouskavachi's death. To what? It occurred to me that this was the same impression I had had of her at Indian Rock yesterday, the sense that it was her nature to be hiding something. "How are you holding up?" I asked.

She jerked around. Those bushy dark eyebrows lifted in surprise. Then she shook her head. "I thought I would handle this better than I am. It's not like I haven't seen people die, you know. No climber of my class has escaped; we've all seen a friend take one wrong step. One minute he's in front of you, pulling out his ice ax, the next moment he's gone. You step wrong on a mountain top and it can be half a mile straight down before you stop. You're dead before you realize what's happened." She shrugged. "Or at least that's what we tell each other. Maybe your screams for help are choked in a throat paralyzed by terror and you can't do anything but watch yourself plunge down picking up speed with each hundred feet till you crash into the rocks thousands of feet below. We won't know till it's too late, will we?" She shrugged again, stiffly this time. "Death is part of mountaineering. It's essential to it. The ultimate danger. If there wasn't the threat of death, there'd be no point in climbing."

I sat on a redwood bench and motioned her across from me, not wanting to break the spell of her introspection. Her soliloquy on death was definitely not part of her public performances, like the one I'd seen two days ago. This was not talk of the ultimate thrill of standing on ice-covered rock on which no human had set foot. Or the wordless bonding between team members who must ultimately depend on each other. Or even the physiological high that comes from great exertion at high elevation, a runner's high doubled and redoubled.

"How do you deal with that?" I asked.

She leaned forward, tan, sleekly muscled arms resting on thighs that showed sinews even in rest. "You know, it's the underside that makes the game worthwhile. If the mountains weren't dangerous they would have been climbed centuries ago. There'd be no bonding of team members, no need for it. It's the danger that weeds out the weak. It's what makes us climbers an elite corps. Nowadays, how many people get the chance to risk everything, betting their own planning, skill, bodies, and snap judgments against the biggest mountains in the world? And knowing there is no chance of rescue? When a friend dies on a mountain it sends a chill so icy through your body that you can't do anything but stand and shiver. You know it could have been you, that the odds are some day it *will* be you. Then you stop shivering and go on, because the next mountain is that much more valuable."

"What about a death like this, dying not on a mountain but on a chaise lounge in town?"

In the pale light I could see the skin on her face tightening. "Death is death. You can't go around assigning values to kinds of deaths, ten points for those who fall off the top of Everest, nine from the top of K-2, one for a guy squashed by an Oakland Scavenger truck on Shattuck

Avenue. Life's a chance. Sometimes you win; eventually you don't. But you can't wallow around thinking about that, right? Cops get shot. It could be you, right?"

It wasn't the same, but there was no value in going into that. I said, "I need to go over a few points in the statement you gave Officer Heling." I asked her about the events of the previous night. "You went to bed at eleven? Downstairs?"

"That's where my room is. That's where I sleep. Alone. Did Brouck try to tell you something different?"

"No," I said. "Has he misled people?"

"I don't know. Maybe he hasn't. But if someone assumed I was more than a guest, I wouldn't count on Brouck setting them straight," she added with a visible shiver.

"What happened after you got down there?"

"Nothing. I didn't hear anything. My room is beneath the first floor."

"Yours permanently?"

"Yes. Mine. Brouck hates it. There's no view but the tree trunks and the hillside brush. He'd use it for storage if I weren't in it. I need a place to keep my stuff when I'm here. Climbing is a poor-man's game. You have to hustle to get backers, to get clothing manufacturers to give you parkas in return for being the 'official parkas of the first mixed-sex Himalayan expedition led by a woman,' to get airlines to contribute free flights, to get ice ax manufacturers—"

"I get the picture."

Her shaggy brows lowered a millimeter. Clearly, Bev Zagoya was used to talking down to people, or perhaps just to other women. As clearly, she was not used to being stopped in midsentence. "The point I'm making, *Detective*, is that I don't have the money to pay rent on a house all year when I'm gone over half of it. This year alone I've been in the Alps twice, on a lecture tour in New England, and given a couple of climbing seminars in Yosemite."

"And Dr. Diamond lets you live here solely because he's fond of you."

"What does he get in return, if not my love? He gets something a lot more satisfying: my reflected glory. Look, I'm no fool. Being a climber is like being poet laureate. In order to write an epic you have to dish out the occasional shit about the queen's birthday. Occasionally I dish myself out at Brouck's dinners with Brouck's friends, and with the hotshot film hopefuls who've spent so much time in L.A. that if they saw a real mountain, they'd be looking around for the freeway tunnel."

For the first time I felt a pang of sympathy for Hasbrouck Diamond, his cherished passion so casually tossed aside. But that pang was brief as I recalled how careless he had been of his neighbor's involvement with him. As I had about Mr. Kepple and his neighbor, I thought how well suited this threesome here was, and how appalled each one of them would be to hear it. Careful to keep a neutral tone, I said, "You were telling me what happened this morning."

"I heard the thud. I looked out my window; it was dark. I didn't see anything."

"What time was it?"

She shrugged. "Still night. I don't have one of those clocks that glows in the dark."

"What did you do?"

She shrugged again. "Went back to sleep."

"You went back to sleep!"

"Well, hell, this is a noisy place."

I pressed my arms against my sides to counter the chill. "After you went back to sleep, what?"

"Nothing till I heard the scream. The woman in the house downhill spotted Kris. I woke up, saw the light from her flashlight, saw something—I couldn't make out that it was Kris then. I ran upstairs and onto the deck. The woman wasn't screaming anymore. She was just standing there, over Kris, staring. I went down Brouck's rappelling wall. I looked at Kris. He was dead. I've seen enough climbing accidents to know death. Then I called the cops. And that's it."

"There must be another way down besides the rappelling rope." By using it, Zagoya had created good reason for her footprints, fingerprints, clothing fibers to be around the spot where Kris went off the deck.

"I wasn't looking for *alternate routes*. My friend was dead. There's a special bond when you climb together. It's not just between the climbers, it's the whole team. Your life depends on everyone on that team. Your victory is their victory. What you feel for each other is like friendship boiled down to its essence. I saw Kris down there. I grabbed the rope and went."

I let a moment pass. The fog had paled to a heather gray. It still clung to the tops of pines and eucalypts. A thin layer spread over the Berkeley flatlands and thickened up at the Bay. San Francisco was beyond, entirely hidden.

"Dr. Diamond thinks Leila Sandoval mistook Kris sleeping on that chaise lounge for him."

She laughed, at first sarcastically, then hysterically. I let her go on, vaguely wondering about all those deaths she'd seen on mountains. When she had control of herself, she said, "Look, they're bonkers, both of them, Brouck and Leila. Is Brouck saying Leila pushed Kris over the edge because she thought it was him, because she was pissed off about him having her trees topped two years ago?"

"Are you saying you don't think she would have?"

"No," she said slowly. "Not exactly."

"Not because of the trees?" When she nodded, I went

on. "What about this affair between them? How serious was Leila? A great passion?"

She laughed, but it was a controlled sound. "Maybe, maybe not. I barely knew Leila then. She didn't talk about it then. And afterward she didn't talk to me at all."

"So she was angry?"

"Oh, yes. She's still angry. She didn't order the bees so I could have honey on my toast. Maybe she was angry about losing Hasbrouck. Maybe he was the great love of her life . . ."

"Or?" I prompted.

"Or maybe she was pissed that her husband left her and she suddenly found herself with no lover, and worse yet, no income."

It made a good motive for trying to kill Diamond. "If this is true," I said, "both you and Dr. Diamond could still be in danger. As long as Leila Sandoval is free. Who might she be staying with? Where?" She started to shake her head. "Think."

She gazed not toward the Golden Gate, but up at the hills. A hazy yellow halo outlined the tops. Sun shining in Orinda and Moraga on the other side. "She may still have some land in Humboldt County," she said with an even tone that belied the impression she was clearly trying to give—that this thought had just risen in her mind. "She got ten acres in her divorce settlement. I don't know whether she still has it."

"Where in Humboldt County?"

She shrugged.

She knew; I would have put money on it. And she'd tell me if I could give her the chance to do it gracefully. I said, "How did she refer to it when she mentioned it? A few acres near—?"

"Near Garberville." She smiled.

I smiled. Garberville was the address Kris Mouskava-chi had had in his pocket.

13

LEONARD had checked in with Martinez fifteen minutes before. The neighbor who had a view of the deck had told Leonard that she had not noticed any blanket-covered body on the chaise; *she* was not in the habit of looking at Diamond's deck, and if she had been in the habit and had seen a covered body, she wouldn't have speculated about who it was, she would only have been relieved that it was neither naked nor creating noise.

I drove back to the station, through the empty early morning streets of Saturday. It was only about six-thirty. Wally's Donuts, my standard breakfast hangout, was open but I didn't feel up to being lectured on my eating habits. Instead, I opted for the hope that the desk man at the station would still have a couple of unclaimed jellies, or maybe a chocolate old-fashioned. And after my night in Mr. Kepple's hospital room, which seemed like weeks ago, and dealing with Kris's death, I was past the point of differentiating between good and bad coffee. The stuff we had in the machine would be fine.

Perhaps it would have been. But the coffee machine was empty (an indicator that there were guys at the station with greater tolerance or less taste than I). And worse yet, when I checked with Sabec at the front deck, he was out of doughnuts.

Pereira was at the desk she shared with patrol officers from the other shift. I relayed Bev Zagoya's speculation about Leila Sandoval hiding on her property near Garberville, and gave her the address Kris had had in his pocket. "Tell the sheriff up there we'll owe him one if he can get us something this morning."

I made my way to my own office. Later in the day, or on a weekday, Howard would be in there, his chair swiveled back to his own desk, his long legs stretched across the floor, feet braced against my desk. Seeing him here would have eased the grayness of this day. But it was not yet seven A.M. Howard was probably still curled up in his extra-long bed, in the forest green bedroom that was the prize awarded to the longest-standing tenant in his house. I sank into my chair, turned toward my desk and began the tedious process of trying to get through to Kathmandu. Getting a free line took half an hour. Not surprisingly the Mouskavachis didn't have a phone in their home. The phone I reached was in a store. The line crackled. Not surprisingly, the man who answered spoke English with a heavy accent, and it was twenty minutes before I understood that he was sending a boy to fetch one of the Mouskavachis.

While I waited, I used another line to call one of the few people I would dare expect to answer the phone civilly at this hour of the morning, Vikram Patel at the Indian consulate in San Francisco. Berkeley has a growing population from India and Nepal whose foreign affairs India handles, and many Berkeleyans have been to India. The result is that I'd had a number of conversations with the personnel at that consulate. And since Delhi time was almost twelve hours different from ours, Vikram Patel was forced to keep peculiar hours. When I told him of Kris's death, Patel, the most courteous of men, expressed proper dismay. Then he paused so long I wondered if the line to San Francisco had been infected by static on my other line to Nepal. Finally, he said, "I do not wish to speak unkindly of the bereaved. I myself do not know the family, but I have heard of them. Often. From my associates in Delhi. They have seen them, often."

"And they have said," I prompted.

"They have described the mother dogging them like a beggar whining for baksheesh."

I sighed. "Poor Kris."

Patel sighed. "I have not met the unfortunate man. But at least he had a few weeks of normal life. I have met the woman who sent him the ticket to come to this country."

"The woman?" Kris had told me Diamond brought him over. Bev Zagoya had told me that too. Diamond couldn't have sent Bev to handle the arrangements because she was in the Alps when Kris came. "Mr. Patel, do you recall what the woman looked like?"

"Sorry. No."

"Rats."

"But I do have her name. Here it is. Leila Sandoval."

"Leila Sandoval! Mr. Patel, can you be sure it was she, not someone using her name?"

"Ah yes, she applied for a visa. So, you see, I saw her and her passport. I am trying to recall her face . . . I cannot."

I thanked Patel, hung up the phone, and got hold of Martinez. "Do you have someone who can bring Bev Zagoya down here now?"

"Leonard's just leaving."

"Thanks."

The Kathmandu call came through. The static was heavy. It took me five minutes to convey my message to Kris's mother, and another five to get from her confirmation that her son's ticket had indeed come from Leila Sandoval. In another three minutes I was satisfied that she probably didn't know why an American woman had sent Kris a ticket, that she assumed the woman was connected to Bev Zagoya since she remembered that Bev lived in California. In the final minute she explained that she had four younger children to occupy her, and assumed that the city of Berkeley would be paying for Kris's funeral.

I had just put the phone down when it rang. Leonard had Zagoya in the interview room.

The interview room is at the far end of the station. Scarred pine tables form a square in the middle. Early in the mornings we hold meetings there. Later we keep "responsibles" in the holding cells that look in on it. Now the room was empty but for Zagoya, still in her yellow shirt and red running shorts, sitting on a pine chair, staring at the wall clock, scowling.

Seeing me her scowl deepened. Before she could speak I said, "Not an hour ago, I told you I wanted the truth. I meant the entire truth, not just what tidbits you chose to toss out. Hasbrouck Diamond didn't bring Kris to this country. That wasn't Leila Sandoval's big favor to mountaineering, having *him* bring Kris over. She paid his way herself. Why didn't you tell me?"

I expected anger, or even sheepishness, but Bev Zagoya looked up at me in surprise. "I didn't think it mattered."

"In a murder investigation everything matters."

She hesitated only momentarily. "It was supposed to be a big secret. Leila swore Kris to secrecy. That amused Kris. Leila herself is no secret keeper, but she would have kept this one. She would have loved to put one over on Brouck."

"*Would have loved?* Are you saying Diamond knew she brought Kris here?"

"Oh, yeah."

"How did he find out?"

Bev Zagoya looked at me as if I were the village idiot. "Kris told him."

Kris had begged me not to tell Diamond he even knew Leila Sandoval. I remembered him lowering his voice, looking at me with those pale blue eyes of his. Had he been lying to me? That possibility shouldn't have surprised me. Still, I found myself surprised . . . and offended. I had to force myself to take the possibility seriously. Or, of course, maybe the one lying was Bev. "Why would Kris have admitted being in the enemy camp?"

She shook her head, "I wasn't there. I was in the Alps then. I don't know what went on."

I sat heavily on the edge of the table and this time made no effort to restrain my disgust. "Don't tell me you came back, heard about Leila paying for Kris's ticket, and you never so much as asked why? No one's that incurious."

Lieutenant Davis, the morning watch commander, opened the glass door to his office and headed across the room. Zagoya followed each step with her eyes. When he disappeared onto the stairs she looked back at the wall clock, scowled again, and said, "I don't know why Leila brought Kris here. Kris didn't know. But Kris was a kid with an eye for a chance and he took it. Then Brouck realized what a plus Kris could be in promoting my new expedition and—well, you know how Brouck and Leila are—he co-opted Kris."

"And Leila was so put out that she killed Kris before he could perform?" A trace of sarcasm came through, but only a trace. With what I'd heard of Sandoval I couldn't rule out that kind of reaction. Zagoya didn't answer; she stared angrily at the wall clock, as if she begrudged every second that ticked by. I pressed her for leads to Sandoval's whereabouts. I asked about my only other possibility of a lead, the boy with the tattoo, but Zagoya swore she knew nothing about him.

She sat glaring at the clock, and I was so irritated at her attitude, I was tempted to drag out her stay here. As it was I restrained the urge to comment on her busy schedule or her exemplary ability to concentrate—at least on our clock.

I looked down from our clock to her empty wrist. A watch was not something a mountaineer would do without. When you're working your way up a mountain face and there are only so many daylight hours left, your life depends on knowing the time. And clearly, she had not done without one. Her tan outlined the place where a watch had been. "Where's your watch?" I asked, suspecting the answer before she said it.

She jerked her eyes away from the clock. "Kris," she said, looking distinctly uncomfortable. "I gave it to him." She forced a smile. "I didn't want to. But you know how Kris was. He loved it, he wanted it. He'd had so little, it was hard to refuse him. It was sort of a celebration of his coming here." Standing, she said, "I feel a little awkward about asking this, but when you're through with the investigation, I would like to have it back. I just bought it in Switzerland. It was an expensive watch."

I let her go, and walked back into my office. It was still early, but not too early to call the hospital. I dialed and got through to the nurses' station nearest Mr. Kepple's room. Mr. Kepple didn't have a phone. The report on his condition was "resting comfortably." Nothing more. I asked the nurse to ask Mr. Kepple about the boy with the tattoo. "That boy was in his Trees class, in gardening," I added. "Ask him what the boy's name is, and see if he has any idea where I might find him."

She put me on hold. It took almost as long as calling Kathmandu for her to return. "Sorry to keep you waiting. It took me a while to get an answer to your question."

I could believe that.

. "I'm afraid Mr. Kepple doesn't know where to find your friend. He says that Cypress—that's his name, you know, like the tree—"

Like the tattoo.

"—he never finished the class. Mr. Kepple seemed to think he was thrown out of the school."

"Why?"

"He didn't say."

"Can you ask him?"

"Doctor came in while I was there. He's with him now. I couldn't interrupt."

"Thanks."

I called Howard. I woke him up. It was still not quite eight in the morning. "I need a favor."

"Some people say 'Good Morning.' "

"I'm a police detective. That is good morning."

"I missed you last night."

Despite the fact that there was no one else in my tiny office, I lowered my voice. "Me, too." Then I told him about Mr. Kepple and his hospitalization, and his observation about Cypress.

Howard laughed. I could picture him propped on an elbow in the middle of his double bed, the tuft of red hairs on his bare chest matted from the night, the door to the balcony that overlooked the back yard open despite the cold fog outside. It was a nice room. Dark green walls, white molding, with big windows letting in the sunlight that filtered through the live oak tree in the back yard. No wonder Howard loved his house. No wonder he was hurt that I didn't. Maybe I should . . . I reminded myself of its other attributes: the sounds of jazz, rock, television, barking dogs, a baying beagle who paced along the upstairs gallery as if each room were inhabited by rabbits, and the screams of lovers and ex-lovers in one or more of the other five bedrooms coming through the walls at any hour of night.

"And so, Detective," Howard said, "you figure that there aren't too many reasons why a guy gets thrown out of a government-sponsored gardening class, right? And you want to trade off my associations in Vice and Substance Abuse and have me check my sources and see if Cypress was dealing."

"That and a local address for him."

"Okay. But this'll cost you."

I smiled. "How much?"

"Come by and see." Some place in the house the beagle bayed.

I could feel the tension in his silence, the tension that was always there now when he coupled a lascivious proposition with an invitation to his house. In my mind, the one detracted from the other. But I wasn't sure Howard was clear on that. And this was hardly the time to comment on the infuriating whines, whistles, and screechings in that house he loved so, as opposed to the seductive appeal of his sleekly muscled chest with its light mat of sun-goldened hairs, or his cute little butt. Quickly, I said, "This is the oddest homicide I've ever had," falling into our sure-fire way of handling awkwardness. "There's the squabble. Now I find that Leila Sandoval paid for Kris Mouskavachi to come to this country. Why? This is a woman who exited a divorce with no money. And then she spends a thousand dollars to fly a strange kid over here."

"How did she even know he existed?" Howard asked. There was no hesitancy in his voice. It was one of his charming qualities this ability to throw himself wholeheartedly into the problem under discussion.

"So she brings him here, Howard, and then he defects to Diamond."

"Nice kid."

"But, Howard, Kris was still hedging his bet. Diamond offered to loan him money for college, he gave him his nicest guest room, and how did Kris react? Kris put not one personal item in that room. He didn't even sleep there. He slept on the deck."

Took his money and scorned his house. Kris knew how to hit Diamond where it hurt, huh?"

I swallowed. "Yeah," I said, but the word was barely audible. I wasn't sure Howard had heard it at all, much less understood that I had caught the personal implications.

The beagle bayed. For once I was thankful. I said, "I'll talk to you later."

I could hear Howard's quick intake of breath. "Where you off to now?"

"To get another man out of bed."

14

MAYBE Howard would find Cypress. Maybe Cypress would lead me to Leila Sandoval. But I couldn't wait. It was time for my one trump card: Herman Ott.

I headed for Ott's office. Patrol hadn't reported a sighting, but I was familiar enough with Ott to know he could have gotten back unseen into the two rooms that housed his office and himself.

Amazingly, it was not quite eight A.M. My reward for starting the day at 4:37.

Two hours from now, Telegraph Avenue would be bustling with students making their way to more civilized ten A.M. classes, or even more civilized cafes, with shop owners unlocking doors and street sellers unfolding card tables and display cases. But now the sidewalk held only two undergraduates running in tandem, clutching notebooks, and a street person who had been an Avenue regular longer than I'd been on the force. He was easing himself up from the vestibule of the pizza shop next to Herman Ott's building. The fog clouded the shop windows and blurred the signs; there was a black-and-white quality to the street.

I could have driven another thirty yards down Tele-graph Avenue and parked in a red zone. Instead I left the patrol car double-parked in front of Herman Ott's build-ing. I was tempted to turn the pulser lights on, but I didn't want to overdo it.

I made my way up the staircase and turned left into the hallway that formed a square around it. As I passed the other "offices" the rhythm picked up and I caught bursts of high-pitched television voices and frenetic music from Saturday morning cartoons, and giggles of the chil-dren watching them.

Ott's two-room office and home was at the end of the hall. As always, the office door was closed. The other room, I knew from my numerous visits here, contained a cot, hot plate, a chair with springs springing, and a homogeneous pile of clothes, sheets, and half-read news-papers that made walking across the floor akin to travers-ing the pasture at the end of mud season. The door was nailed shut. But Ott was in there, I was ninety percent sure of that. With his clientele Ott wasn't likely to leave his office untended long enough for word to get around. Ott was not a morning person. By nature he was not even a day person. With the same fervor with which a body-builder nurtures muscles and a year-round tan, Ott main-tained his sallow complexion. Right now, he'd be lying under a heap of yellow blankets on the cot. He was in there all right. But if I knocked on the door, he'd never answer.

I stepped softly down the hall to the nailed-closed door, bent down, poked open the mail slot, and stuck my ear next to it. No snores. He probably even had his nose under the yellow blankets. Probably all of him that was visible was a few greasy strands of blond hair. I rattled that door handle as loud as I could, and listened. A groan.

Behind me, across the hall, a door squeaked open. A

young woman peered out. I smiled. She shrugged. She might well want to warn Ott, but it was too late for that.

I pushed Ott's mail slot in and let it bang back. In and bang. In and bang. Then I rattled the handle again. I smacked both hands against the door and ran loudly down the hall in my best imitation of the mischievous children that Ott had grumbled about. It wasn't an Academy Award performance, but then Ott wasn't exactly awake, either.

I was rewarded with a grunt.

It took three more runs through the whole routine before I could hear Ott cursing and clambering up and heading for the door in the office. He flung it open, and before he could get both feet out into the hall I was inside.

He glared at me. "What the hell— You! Hey, you have a warrant or something?"

I held up my hand. "Skip it, Ott." I settled on the edge of his desk. "I don't have time for amenities. We have a common goal here."

"No, we don't, Smith. My only goal is to get you out of here and get back to bed. Unless you'd like to join me there."

I stared at Ott. Mustard-colored sweatpants spanned his round belly and flapped around his skinny legs. A lemon-and-ochre-swirl turtleneck came down not quite far enough to camouflage a burst of pale fuzz in the neighborhood of where his waist might have been. His thin blond hair lay plastered to his head except for one greasy clump that poked out above his left ear, and his eyes were so caked with sleep it looked like the sandman had dumped his whole load and taken the rest of the night off. "Ott," I said, "the sight of you in the morning would be enough to make a lesser woman turn to sheep."

"Out!"

"The Sandoval case—it's murder now."

Ott had been about to repeat his order. Instead, he

twisted his fists around his eyes. I knew he was using the time to try to figure who might have been killed, and what his own reaction should be. I gave him a full sixty seconds; I needed him awake.

"Who?" he asked.

"Kris Mouskavachi."

A small shiver rippled down Ott's flesh. It was a big reaction for Herman Ott, who prided himself on never reacting, never getting personally involved, and above all, never giving anything away. That shiver revealed more than half an hour of questioning would have drawn out. A fairer person might have told him that Hasbrouck Diamond might have been the intended victim. I didn't; I went with the advantage of that shiver. "Leila Sandoval is in the middle of this. And she's still not home."

"So find her, Smith. You're a hotshot detective."

"Ott, I don't have time to run through our usual song and dance. I've got a call in to Humboldt County. It's only a matter of time before we bring Cypress in, and Cypress ties you into Sandoval and that performance on the street yesterday. Do I make myself clear?" I didn't know whether Ott had been a party to Sandoval's escape, or if she'd used him. For the moment it made no difference; Ott would be more likely to deal with the consequences of the former than admit the latter.

Ott leaned back against the door. He muttered, "You got nothing, Smith." Then he waited. I knew that look: puffy eyelids half closed over deep-set hazel eyes. It meant: Make me an offer.

But I wasn't about to deal, not on this one. "Ott, let me put it in the terms of those volleyball games you like to watch so much. The woman spiked me. She spiked me, but *you* gave her the lay-up to do it."

Ott relaxed back against the edge of the door. It wavered from side to side.

I stepped forward, grabbed the door above Ott's

head, and slammed it shut. As Ott jerked forward and bobbled for his balance on the balls of his surprisingly long narrow feet, I said, "Sandoval's got land in Humboldt County. Maybe she's there. Maybe she's hiding out with someone in Berkeley. I don't care. You see that she is here by noon."

Ott just stared. "Or?"

"Look out your window."

With a shrug of his spongy sloping shoulders, he sidled to the window. The panes hadn't started as opaque glass, but years of external neglect by the building manager and internal neglect by Ott himself had turned them a mold-speckled gray. Ott had to raise the window to peer out down the alley to the small slice of street he could view.

"You see the black-and-white parked down there? The pulser light's off now. At twelve-oh-one it'll be on. At twelve-oh-two there'll be a patrol officer outside your door, calling to you. If you go out our guys will be waving to you."

Ott slammed the window and turned toward me. "Smith, you need me to define harassment?"

"We're not talking harassment. Just friendly attention, just so your associates know that we on the force are pleased to see you."

Ott's sallow face turned orange. If there was one thing Herman Ott valued it was his reputation of never cooperating with the police unless there was no way of avoiding it, and never admitting anything about a client. It was his pride, and it probably explained why a guy as out of shape as he was had survived as long as he had, and had gotten paid enough to live, even in the fashion to which he was naturally accustomed. "I don't know where she is."

"Find her."

He rocked slowly back and forth on those long feet, thinking. It was a move of his I hadn't seen before, one I couldn't interpret.

114

"Find her, Ott."

He stopped moving and stared down at his feet. "Look, Smith, I'm going to give you the truth. I liked Kris; he was a good kid in his way."

I waited to hear the rest of his assessment of Kris. I couldn't believe Herman Ott had missed the "to the highest bidder" quality in the boy.

But if he caught it, he didn't mention it. Still eyeing his pedal digits he said, "The truth is, Smith, that I don't know where Leila Sandoval is. And I have no idea how to find her."

"Ott!" I exclaimed. "I'm, well, *insulted* that you would expect me to buy that. Come on!"

He threw up his hands. His yellow sleeves nearly covered them.

"Your client and you don't know where to find her?"

"She's not my client."

"She has been, though, hasn't she?" Ott was not one to bestow unpaid favors on acquaintances, like coming to their defense and letting them escape the police. But once a person had become his client, once he'd taken her under his professional wing, he seemed to feel an ongoing responsibility. This was not to say he would take cases for nothing; he wouldn't. "Smith, I said I was giving you the truth. I don't know where she is."

I sat back on the edge of his big wooden desk, considering my options. Why would Sandoval have hired a private detective? How long ago? Would that reason have anything to do with this case? That was information I definitely would not get out of Ott. Still, what *was* the woman involved in? I was tempted to tell him that I already knew about her bringing Kris over from Nepal. But something stopped me. Instead, I said, "Be that as it may, Ott, you do understand it is in her best interest to turn herself in. It is in my best interest. And it is definitely in your best interest to get her here by noon."

Ott stood motionless, still staring down at his calloused feet. "I'll give you a gift."

Words I'd never before heard from Herman Ott. I waited.

Still avoiding my gaze, he said, "I can't have her here this morning. No way. I'll do what I can to contact her, because, as you said, it's in her best interest. Leila Sandoval is no killer."

"What kind of gift—"

"Hey, keep your pants on, Smith. This gift may save you days of running after an innocent woman."

I nodded warily. Ott fingered the edge of the phone directory, the business pages.

"Kris died at Brouck Diamond's place, right?"

I nodded, making a mental note of the familiar way he referred to the periodontist.

"Also in that house is Beverly Zagoya, the mountaineer, right?"

And a woman whom he mentioned in formal style. I nodded.

"Do you know what the inside word was on her last expedition?"

"According to Kris?"

Ott's shoulders tightened. Now *I* had insulted *him.* "According to more than Kris. I don't take things on faith, Smith."

"Right."

"On that expedition, which Zagoya led, three people died."

"Three out of how many?" I recalled Kris Mouskavachi saying that ten percent of mountain climbers die routinely.

"Ten. But that's not the point, Smith. The point is that they were taking a route they should never have taken. They were going across part of the mountain where there were avalanches every hour or so."

"Every hour?"

"That's the word. You want the rest or not?" Ott was still avoiding my gaze.

"Go on."

"They tried to time the avalanches, to make their way across the face right after one. But there's no way to know for sure. Once they got to a certain spot on the open face, there was no turning back, and no cover. The next avalanche came early. It knocked the last three, one American and two Sherpas, a couple of thousand feet straight down." He sidled over to the window and stared out, as if to focus on any scene other than the one he was describing, an abnormally squeamish reaction for Herman Ott. It was a moment before the real cause of his squeamishness clicked in with me; he wasn't avoiding the picture of the avalanche, it was this scene here he couldn't face, the scene in which he was giving, *giving* a police detective information.

I leaned back, eyeing Ott. His shoulders hunched, one foot tapped irregularly, and the loose cotton of his sweatpants ruffled like feathers in a storm. Ott looked as uncomfortable as I had ever seen him. A lot more uncomfortable than this comparatively innocuous bit of information warranted. "Ott, climbers die. It's a fact of the sport."

He slammed the window shut and spun to face me. "Do I have to spell it out for you? Okay. *A*: there was a safer route. *B*: that route was longer. *C*: the expedition didn't have enough supplies to take the safer route. Because, *D*: Zagoya didn't plan well enough. Got it?"

"But Ott, there are a lot of variables—"

Ott was actually shaking. "Smith, the woman cut corners buying food. *Food*, for Chrissakes. Everyone told her what she had wasn't enough; she wouldn't listen. There's no second chance up there. They don't have Seven-Elevens on the top of the Himalaya. She as good as killed those three people."

15

WHEN I got back to the office, Howard was sitting facing into the room, the yard or more of his legs sprawled across it, his feet resting against my desk. On the edge of his desk sat Pereira, *her* feet propped on his lower drawer, her chin covered with powdered sugar.

"Where'd you find that doughnut? Has Sabec gotten a new supply?" Still eyeing her sugared chin, I demanded, "You didn't eat the last one, did you?" I stepped over Howard's shins, and dropped into my chair.

"I'm young, and blond, and upwardly mobile," Pereira said, wiping the sugar off her face. "I have everything to live for. I wouldn't throw it all away for the last doughnut when I know you're going to show up."

"Sabec's empty. Not a doughnut in the box. Not a cruller in the station. Not a chocolate old-fashioned for blocks around." Howard leaned forward and opened my bottom drawer. "But there is one jelly." He pulled out a napkin-wrapped mound.

I unwrapped. "Ah, Howard. You're a fine man."

"Finer than you think." He extricated a thermos and poured. The smell of Peet's coffee floated up.

"Better than a mother," Pereira said, patting Howard's shoulder.

Into my mouth I stuffed the edge of the doughnut, the part where the jelly went in, and would, given the chance, squirt out. I had had experience, or rather *experiences* with jelly holes. Still chewing, I motioned Pereira to report on her findings.

"Oh, no, Smith. Martinez said you were off to see everyone's favorite private eye. You get nothing before you tell us about that."

Howard grinned. "You keep up your record, Jill?"

My little niche of fame within the department was for getting more information out of Herman Ott than anyone else on the force, small amount that that was. I took another bite of doughnut and nodded.

Howard and Pereira sat and watched me chew.

"Okay, okay," I said, putting the remaining half down, "but if all the jelly drips out while I'm talking you'll both be in deep . . . jelly." With that I recounted what Herman Ott had told me about the three deaths on the Zagoya expedition.

"So what happened? Did you let him off the hook about producing Sandoval?" Pereira demanded.

I took a long drink of coffee, savoring the first invigorating swallow. "Giving a gift of information to his local police department was a wrenching experience for citizen Ott." I took another drink. The second swallow is never as good as the first. But it was still pretty darned good. "A finer person," I said, eyeing Howard, "might have taken that into account."

"A finer person who is not a homicide detective?" he asked.

I nodded.

"So, as Lout of the Day, you—"

"Amended my order and told him to get her in here by five." I took another bite of doughnut, a small one, so

119

I could talk with my mouth only partially full. "He was straight about not knowing her whereabouts; I'm sure of that. It was so humiliating for him to admit it. And besides, I figured by now you"—I eyed Pereira—"would have gotten me a lead from the Humboldt County guys."

"And I have." Pereira reached out a hand for my coffee cup, took a long swallow, and smiled. "And lots, lots more. Sandoval owns ten acres outside Garberville. At the address Kris Mouskavachi had in his pocket." Pereira took another swallow of my coffee. Pereira had her own niche of fame in the department. Jackson had nicknamed her Spot, after his food-scarfing dog who was no longer allowed near the dinner table. "But you won't need to visit that property, because the Humboldt sheriff's department sent a man out and found Sandoval sitting in the sun on her porch. He is only too happy to have us pay for a weekend trip down to Berkeley. So, Smith, you will have Sandoval in your office before Herman Ott realizes it's daytime."

"Not half bad for a morning's work," I said appreciatively.

"Wait!" Pereira was grinning. "According to the sheriff the neighbors said there was a youngish man living on the property. Said his name was Cypress."

"Is the sheriff bringing him, too?"

"You don't want much, do you?"

"Well?"

"No," she said. "He's gone. Wandered out into the back forty."

Now it was Howard who was smiling.

To him, I said, "Do I take that smile to mean that under the mighty Cypress a little grass did grow, and change hands locally?"

"Humboldt County's biggest cash crop, Jill. Our associates from the state Campaign Against Marijuana Planting were already on to him."

I put the rest of my doughnut in my mouth and chewed thoughtfully. In Berkeley, marijuana is very low priority. Vice and Substance Abuse has coke and crack to deal with, drugs that lead to vicious muggings and drive-by shootings. But in Humboldt County it's a different story. And with the pressure from CAMP, growing ten acres of marijuana up there could be a very risky business—a business to which Cypress was not likely to return, at least not soon enough to be any use to me. But as the owner of the property he had planted, Leila Sandoval had put herself in a dicey position. And that would be useful.

Howard must have been thinking the same thing. He said, "They don't massage feet in the federal pens."

To Pereira, I said, "How about her finances? Could she maintain a life in the hills on feet alone?"

Pereira finished my coffee, looked irritably at the empty cup and plopped it proprietorially in Howard's trashcan. "Getting a banker's assessment of a private account without a warrant is not an easy thing to do, Smith. And on Saturday morning, you're asking your tame banker to make a special trip into the office."

"Which you did, right?"

Pereira smiled. The world of stocks and bonds and margin calls fascinated Connie Pereira. While Howard and I swam laps or, as the case had become more frequently, *didn't* swim laps, Connie Pereira dipped into *A Survey of the History of Pork Belly Strategies*. "Am I correct, Smith, in assuming that you figure Sandoval to be poor and Diamond richish?"

"Right."

"Wrong. Or at least partly. Diamond, it seems, is pretty much living week to week—"

"Or gum job to gum job," Howard put in.

"He refinanced his house a year ago to the tune of

121

three hundred thousand. He bought heavily before the last crash—"

"In the stock market?"

Pereira nodded briskly. "He's backing a film company, enough to drive any banker or broker to drink, and slicing up gum tissue to keep a roof over his head and suntan lotion on his body."

"And Sandoval?"

Pereira sighed, looking around as if expecting to find a new platter from which to appropriate food as she dispensed her findings, and thus maintain an equilibrium of sorts. She sighed again. "She used to work in public relations on and off. But for a number of years right after her divorce—I can't say how many, my source figured two, but it could be more—Sandoval really did live hand to mouth. She's lived in that little house on Panoramic Way for years, so her house payment's only three hundred a month."

Howard whistled. The communal *rent* on his house was ten times that.

"Right. With the refinance Diamond's payment is thirty-four hundred a month. But for Sandoval that three hundred was harder to come by than his. She had no income. My source doesn't know how she managed."

"Not public assistance, not with a house worth what that one is," I said.

"It'd take a lot of tired feet to kick in three hundred a month," Howard said, grinning.

Pereira groaned.

Ignoring that, I said, "We'll have to check on how long she's been a working masseuse."

"You don't need to worry about that, Smith," Pereira said, "because a year ago Sandoval got a check for ten thousand, and another one two months ago."

"Signed by?"

"Guess who?"

"Cypress?"

"You got it."

I leaned back against my desk, smiling. "So I guess we know how she managed to pay airfare for Kris Mouskavachi. Now the only question is, why? After all those years of scraping by, why would she spend more than ten percent of her liquid assets to bring a strange boy over from Nepal?"

"Maybe Kris Mouskavachi wasn't a stranger," Howard said. He was smiling, too. This was just the part of the puzzle Howard loved. "After all, Cypress wasn't a stranger. Maybe your masseuse had a thing for nubile toes and arches."

"No down at the heels for her, eh?" Pereira pushed herself up.

"Where are you off to?" I asked.

"I've got a lead on the broker who had handled Diamond's disastrous investments. A friend arranged lunch in Sausalito. I'm going to start charging the department for clothes."

"We've got some spares in our detail. Check with the hooker decoys."

"One does not lunch with a banker in lamé," Pereira announced as she headed for the door.

"Check in when you get back," I said.

"Right."

As the door swung closed, Howard stood up and stretched. "And I, Jill, am going home, to catch up on the sleep you ruined this morning."

"Me? How about your favorite beagle?"

Howard's pause was infinitesimal, but plenty long enough for me to regret that comment, and its unintended derogation of his beloved house. And to note, with a jab of fear, how much easier, more playful, less painful was Howard's sparring with Pereira. I gave a quick listen to rule out approaching footsteps in the hall, stood up on tiptoe, and wrapped my arms around his neck and kissed him. "About last night, I'll make it up to you."

"When?" he said, running both hands down my back and pressing me to him. I could tell he, too, was listening for footsteps.

"As soon as I get Kris's killer. Now, tell me, how good a friend are you?"

Howard sighed, releasing his hold. "Not that good."

"You don't know what I'm going to ask."

"I know that look."

"It'll just be half an hour. You have the whole day off."

"I brought you coffee."

"I'm working a one eight seven. I have to find out about Zagoya and her dead climbers. God knows when I'll get home again."

"I saved you the last doughnut."

"Howard, if you don't help I will be so exhausted for days . . ."

"The ultimate threat!" He leaned back against the edge of his desk. "On the other hand, if you won't get home for days, what difference—"

I rolled up an In Custody report and hit him.

"Police brutality! Okay, what do you want me to do?"

"Water Mr. Kepple's plants."

"What?"

"Look, I haven't seen him since yesterday. I have to fit in a quick visit sometime today. And what do you think will be the first thing he asks me?"

"Right. Consider your ass covered. Alas, figuratively speaking. And have a good time with Zagoya."

Before I could answer, the phone rang. As I reached for it, Howard patted the anatomical area just discussed and headed out the door. I picked up the receiver. "Homicide. Detective Smith."

"Vikram Patel here."

"Mr. Patel? Are you calling about Kris Mouskavachi?"

"Yes." There was an unusual hesitancy to his speech.

"Do you need to know when the coroner will be releasing the body?" I prompted.

"No. No. No, the reason for my call is to, uh, inform you that Mr. and Mrs. Mouskavachi, the parents, contacted my associates in Kathmandu. The news is bad. They were very distressed about their son's death—" His voice didn't drop as it would at the end of a sentence; he simply discontinued speaking.

I waited.

I could hear him taking a breath. "As I said, the news is bad, for you. They are on their way to Berkeley. They are due to arrive tomorrow morning."

"Thank you for informing me. I've already spoken to Mrs. Mouskavachi, but it is always helpful to hold an interview in person. So it won't be all bad." I realized I had fallen into his formal pattern of speech. How had he described the woman? "Like a beggar whining for baksheesh."

There was another pause. "That's good. Because the Mouskavachis have no friends or relations in the city and, of course, very little money. From the airport they are planning to come directly to your police station and they are planning to stay there."

16

I DROVE east to Panoramic Way more quickly than I might have, had I not been thinking about the imminent descent of the elder Mouskavachis. I recalled Kris's description of them sitting around the Kathmandu pie shop hour after hour, day after day, waffling about their half-baked plans to go to Delhi. I recalled stories of families in India who had camped in hospital lobbies for the entire stay of their infirm relatives, and others who had lived in railway stations for generations. It didn't take a vivid imagination to picture the Mouskavachis settling between the curving staircases in the lobby of the Berkeley Police Station, prepared to set up housekeeping with the same paraphernalia with which they had debarked on the Indian subcontinent twenty years ago. And it took no leap of thought to imagine the heat I would get from Inspector Doyle, and the heat he and the chief would get from the newspapers, television stations, city council, and one or more contingents of outraged citizens if we tried to remove forcibly the impoverished and grieving parents of a young man murdered after only six weeks in our city. Even in the great pasture of Berkeley, this would be the

126

carnival of the decade. I squeezed my eyes shut momentarily against the building fatigue, and reminded myself I *had* slept some last night, albeit in a chair.

I stepped harder on the gas.

It was nearly eleven o'clock when I crossed Telegraph Avenue. Unlike yesterday there were no halter-clad strollers glancing at tables of tie-dyed fabric. The tables were there, all right, but the students who hurried past them were clad in down jackets. And the sun that had steamed the sidewalks yesterday was hidden above a canopy of mustardy fog, which gave the city a two-dimensional look. The Berkeley Hills were a quarter of a mile away; I couldn't see them. That odd flash of heat was gone, and the Bay Area was back to normal summer—fog covering the city till eleven or twelve, sun till four when the afternoon winds pushed the fog back in.

I drove on through the uncrowded streets, past the fraternity houses and the football stadium, and turned right by the carriage house at the entrance to Panoramic Way.

The street was clear of patrol cars by now. Martinez and Raksen had gone. The yellow plastic "ropes" had been untied and rolled back up. And Hasbrouck Diamond's deck looked almost normal, if you ignored the broken railing on the side where the eucalyptus branch had hit, and the skid marks by the gateway Kris's chaise lounge had sailed through. I wouldn't have been surprised to see Hasbrouck Diamond sunning himself or, considering the weather, fogging himself in a deck chair. I would have been pleased to find him there, ready to tell me, truthfully for a change, not why Leila Sandoval had spent a thousand dollars to bring a strange boy to this country—after Herman Ott's recitation I could guess that—but why he had decided to take under his wing a boy who could testify to Bev Zagoya's fatal mismanagement on the last expedition she led. Had Diamond assumed he could subvert Kris? Had he, indeed, been able to?

But Diamond was not on his deck. And a couple of rings on the doorbell told me he wasn't home at all. And neither was Bev Zagoya.

"Damn!" I muttered. Where could Diamond be? Depressed as he had seemed hours ago, I couldn't picture him tooling off to Safeway to restock the larder. Nothing suggested he had friends he would turn to for comfort. He could have gone out for brunch, but with Bev's planned reception at the house he must have had food for an army inside. If he were depressed . . . Then I recalled Orchard Lane, the Italianate stairway he had described as a three-minute vacation in Florence.

It was a good description. I had come across Orchard Lane a couple of years ago when I'd been making my way down Panoramic from a walk on one of the fire trails that cut through the dry hillside grass above. How Orchard lane had gotten its unsuitable name was a question I had never found the right person to ask. It is not a lane but one of the many steep hillside staircases or gently inclining paths that cut through long city blocks. It joins two levels of Panoramic Way. Age-cracked cement railings supported by urn-shaped posts run down beside the wide stairs. Tertiary staircases lead off to the side, narrow, and disappear into vine-covered paths between Italianate cottages. I wouldn't have been surprised to hear Gypsy violin music or to see a figure in a Pierrot costume vanishing behind one of those heavy oaken doors.

I walked down twenty steps to a plateau, down another twenty steps to a second and a third, to a cement alcove that must have been the backdrop of a statue. The statue was gone now, but a bench stood beside the empty spot. And on the bench, statuelike himself, sat Hasbrouck Diamond.

Sitting there, clad in brown corduroy slacks and a

thick black sweater, head hanging as always, he didn't seem out of place the way he did on his own deck. His deck was a spot for the young, muscular, well-oiled, tanned stars of the movie company in which he had invested. But Orchard Lane, with the fog weighing down the thick spatulate leaves of loquat trees, and rectangles of yellow light in the house windows serving only to make the lane grayer and colder and more suitable to the solitary griever, here Hasbrouck Diamond seemed at home.

I sat next to him on the bench and without preamble said, "Three people died on the last expedition Bev Zagoya led."

His eyes closed.

"Kris knew that, right?"

Slowly, he nodded.

"What would that do to Bev's trying to get funding for her new expedition?"

He didn't answer.

"What?" I insisted.

He shrugged.

"Answer me!"

"I don't know, dammit. Bev's the one who knows the ins and outs of fund raising."

"We're talking about the woman you are 'very fond and very, very proud' of. Don't tell me you haven't given this threat any thought."

"Listen, it's not that big a thing. Probably it wouldn't make any difference at all. The story's not new. No one in the climbing community is going to be shocked. Climbers are willing to sign on. Climbers love the thrill. And there's no thrill without danger."

That was what Bev had said earlier this morning. Still, that conclusion didn't satisfy me. "There's danger and there's danger. I can believe climbers want to try virgin mountains, that they're willing to face sub-zero temperatures, avalanches, and the knowledge that the climb may be twice as hard and twice as dangerous as they had any right to expect. But I also believe that climbers who survive do as much as possible to shift the odds in their favor. They don't sign on with leaders who are incompetent."

Diamond jerked up. His thin, pale hair flapped against his head. "Incompetent! Beverly is hardly incompetent. Look, what happened to that climber and those Sherpas could have happened to anyone. The Sherpas climb for a living; they live in the Himalaya, for Chrissakes. Bev assumed they'd be careful."

"She put them in a position where they had no choice," I said, hoping that Herman Ott's information was accurate. It always had been. And in his bad position with me, he wouldn't have dared to offer me a rotten lead.

"On a climb like that everyone has a choice. You don't follow orders when the price is your life." Someone not looking for new signs of unease would have missed the slight quiver in Diamond's voice as he started to respond.

"But if your choice is between freezing overnight or chancing an avalanche?" I prodded.

"Then you time the slides and make your move. There's a rhythm to slides. A good climber has to figure it."

That had the ring of a response Diamond had either used or heard used before. And as he gave it he sounded like a climber, an insider—the mark of success for a groupie. I said, "But Bev still needs backing."

Diamond sat up straight. "Look, backers only care about 'now.' If they can back a California expedition that puts a woman leader on the top of Everest, they don't care if half the Sherpas in Nepal died the last time. When pictures of Bev standing on top of Everest with the state flag flapping behind her Evergreen parka hit the front pages, people will flock to Evergreen outlets. And they're not going to be asking who died on the previous expedition. Besides," he said, turning to face me, "why are you asking about this? Why aren't you trying to find that lunatic woman who tried to kill me?"

"Because I have found her. And, Dr. Diamond, I don't think she was trying to kill you at all. I think the killer knew exactly who was on that chaise lounge." I watched for his reaction. Through his tan, his face turned an unpleasant shade of brick. He sputtered, and the sputters led to coughs. "You lied to me, Dr. Diamond."

He was still dealing with the aftermath of the coughs.

"You told me you brought Kris over here. You didn't, and you knew it was Leila Sandoval who paid Kris's air fare. And you could make a good guess just why. The bees she ordered to disrupt Bev's presentation were a poor replacement for Kris telling about the three deaths—that they were caused by Bev's incompetence."

"You're as crazy as she is. I know my rights, I'll call—"

"Inspector Doyle again? It's gone way beyond that."

"I don't have to put up with this." He pushed himself up.

"You do. Sit down. You think that you can do an end run around me, manipulate the newspapers, and create a hassle for the department. But not this time. Murder makes a difference in the way the public views stories. The public was willing to be entertained by your antics over the eucalyptus. They wanted a laugh. They're not going to be laughing about a teenage boy who's dead. This is murder. You are a suspect. No one is impressed by murder suspects kicking up a fuss. It only makes them look suspicious."

He sat.

I continued, "Now tell me about Leila paying to bring him over here."

"Ask her."

"I'm asking *you* why you accepted Kris as a house guest when she brought him to this country."

The twitch at the side of his mouth was probably a small smile, but it was hard to tell at the angle his head was hanging. "Kris was a charming boy. He could have been a great asset at receptions like the one we had planned for today. Bev, well, Bev can be abrupt; she doesn't have the social sense Kris did."

"How did Kris come to stay with you? Or let me rephrase that, Dr. Diamond. What did you offer him to lure him away from Leila Sandoval?"

There was definitely a smile now. "The boy had good taste. It was my house, my lifestyle he wanted to fit into. And, I like to think, he had a certain fondness for me."

"The lure? Specifically, Dr. Diamond?"

That smile vanished. "A loan for college," he muttered.

"College costs ten thousand dollars a year. You couldn't pay that."

"Once we got the backing . . ."

Sleazier and sleazier. Duping the backers? Promising Kris money that might never materialize? But at the same time making damned sure Kris didn't interfere with the fund raising. But Kris was not a kid to be swayed by sleazy pipe dreams. "And what else did you offer him?"

To his navel, he muttered, "Introductions to the CEO of Evergreen equipment."

I almost laughed. Poor Kris, so ruthless and yet so naive. Out of his league with the well-seasoned feuders of Panoramic Way. I glanced at Diamond. Hasbrouck Diamond didn't look like someone who'd been one-upped. He looked smug. "And how were you planning to use Kris to get back at Leila?"

"I didn't know. I figured the perfect move would come to me."

"Like a phone call to CAMP?"

He didn't reply, but his smile returned.

In Sandoval's mind Diamond was probably responsible for her divorce and penury. He had undermined her massage business, forced her out of her home with it, and in all probability had now turned her in on drug charges for renting the land which she might well feel she had to rent because Diamond had so impoverished her. With all that, her pushing Diamond off the deck didn't seem so unbelievable. Pushing Kris off after he turned traitor was suddenly not so out of the question, either.

I left Diamond with instructions to have Bev Zagoya call me. As I walked back up those cement steps, it struck me that the picture Hasbrouck Diamond had presented me here was not unlike Orchard Lane itself, at once real and the stuff of fantasies, and damned hard to figure which is which.

It also struck me that it was nearly noon, that the Humboldt County Sheriff would be arriving with Sandoval in an hour, and that I had sixty minutes to make an appearance in Mr. Kepple's hospital room and get something for lunch. Maybe Mr. Kepple would have an idea where Cypress might stay. When the Humboldt guy brought Leila Sandoval in, it would be a good thing to have something to give him in return.

17

A MORE compassionate person would have visited Mr. Kepple first. A less hungry, more compassionate person. But as soon as I got in the car, hunger grabbed me, and shook me so that I felt that panicky-must-eat feeling. The need for ice cream. Half a pint of Chocolate Marzipan Swirl, or Chocolate Grand Marnier, or a double scoop of Double Dark Chocolate Double Espresso in a chocolate sugar cone—dipped. I stopped at Ortmann's on Solano. And I did consider getting a pint and two dishes and sneaking it into the hospital. About a year into my tenancy, Mr. Kepple and I had discovered our mutual fondness for ice cream (that is, his occasional pleasure in a dish, and my untamed passion). We had sat on the step to my porch-cum-apartment and shared a couple of containers. But the drawbacks were quickly apparent. The sight of the yard was never appealing, and the smell would have inhibited a lesser appetite. And the conversation . . . Even when what went into Mr. Kepple's mouth was Marshmallow Mocha Mint, what came out was a monologue on manure, mulch, and mealy bugs.

I wandered up Solano, licking my Double Double

cone, feeling guilty about not getting ice cream for Mr. Kepple, feeling annoyed that I felt guilty—annoyed that in the middle of a murder case I felt obligated to visit my former landlord, and guilty about being annoyed. The ice cream ran down the side of the cone. With one great swath of tongue I caught it. It dripped out of the bottom. Onto my slacks.

It was one-thirty when I walked into Mr. Kepple's room. I shivered, remembering my fear that he had had a stroke. He didn't look like he had any residual damage. Thirty-six hours ago he had been the color of mashed potatoes. Now he was sitting up in bed, pushing a mound of them around his plate with his fork, while using the other hand to flick the remote control as the television picture jumped from station to station. An I.V. tube still threaded into his arm; his leg, under the sheet, was in a cast. Still, he could have had a stroke, a small stroke. Something had caused him to fall in a yard that he knew better than most people know their living rooms.

Looking at him now, I noted that his round face was surprisingly ruddy for a hospitalized patient, and his gray hair was combed instead of poking out in clumps as it did when he was digging or mowing or just standing in the yard running dirt-encrusted fingers through it.

"Jill," he said, finger still pressing the remote control. "I've got to get out of here."

"It's okay, Mr. Kepple."

"They say they're running tests to find out why I fell. I don't have time for tests. I have—"

I put a hand on his arm. "It's okay. I watered the garden."

"I have to . . . Oh. Did you get the zinnias? What about the cosmos, they shrivel in this kind of heat. Is it as hot as it was yesterday? I can't find the danged weather report on the TV."

135

"The plants are okay. It's not hot today. Look outside at the fog. Tell me how it is you fell."

"But they still need watering."

"Howard's watering. At this very moment he's in your yard with a hose. About your fall—"

"Howard? The big one with all that red hair? He doesn't know plants."

"Mr. Kepple, Howard's doing you a favor!" I almost added, "Any moron can hold a hose." But I caught myself and thus saved fifteen minutes of didacticism on the varying rates of moisture absorption of our local flora.

"The cineraria, are they—"

"Mr. Kepple, it's been less than two days since you were out there," I said before it became obvious that I had no idea which plants the cineraria were. "Now tell me about falling."

I watched him as he considered my question. I knew that expression; he was gauging whether to go on pressing me for more botanical reassurance. And I was assessing him. Were his eyes moving normally? Was he hesitating too long? What were the signs of a small stroke anyway? And what was the prognosis? Would he be a candidate for a bigger one? Would he have to avoid bending over, having the blood rushing to his head? *Not* lift fifty-pound garden sacks? And did it mean that someone would have to keep an eye on him? "Mr. Kepple, how did you feel just before you fell? Lightheaded? Dizzy? Did everything go black?"

He gave me such a puzzled look that I wondered if he was following the conversation. "It was just a fall. I didn't see it and I fell."

Night blindness? A sudden blackout? What did that indicate. "Didn't see what?"

"The wheelbarrow," he said, as if that were *the* item God had created to propel the human body earthward.

"You didn't see it?" I asked, alarmed. "Were you wearing your glasses?"

He nodded.

"When was the last time you had the prescription checked?"

"I don't know, Jill, a couple years ago."

In Kepple-ese, for a nonbotanical task a couple of years could mean a decade. "But, Jill, it was dark."

"Even so," I said, thinking of those antique lenses. "You have lights in the yard."

"Out."

"You took them out!"

"No, no. They're still there. In fact—now, you tell me what you think of this—I was considering replacing them with pole lanterns. I could get colored glass, different colors, some red, some yellow, blue, light blue—"

"About the lights you have now, Mr. Kepple, why weren't they on?"

"Didn't turn them on," he muttered.

"Mr. Kepple, it took you two months to get those lights in the way you wanted them, and now you're not even using them?" Why did this surprise me? "Have you thought of calling an electrician?"

"They work. Didn't turn them on," he said, his voice softer than before.

"Why not?"

"Because there was no moon."

I was leaning forward to make out his words. "You're telling me that you spent weeks of time and God knows how much money to put lights in the yard, and then on a night when there is no moon, when it is pitch black in your backyard, you don't turn those lights on?"

"Wanted it dark."

"Oh." Now light was beginning to dawn. "Why?"

"So they wouldn't see." It was nearly a whisper.

"So *the neighbors* wouldn't see. See what?"

"Pps."

"What?"

"Ppppsss."

I had my ear nearly next to his mouth and still I had a hard time making out the word. "*Pipes*. Garden pipes? Irrigation pipes?"

Mr. Kepple took the TV remote in both hands and made a show of changing the channel. To a soap opera. He straightened his shoulders and said, "Well, Jill, I think the heat has gotten to some of my neighbors. You know they used to be nice people, good neighbors. Oh, some of them don't do much with their yards, but to each his own, that's what I say. I don't hold that against them. Bert Pendergast, now he tries, but that magnolia of his, it hasn't had a blossom in years. Doesn't fertilize, doesn't put anything into the soil. Nothing in, nothing out, that's what I told him."

"And I'm sure he appreciated it," I said, forgetting that sarcasm was lost on Mr. Kepple. "I've been at your house. I know the neighbors complaining about you using too much water."

"I wanted to put a stop to that, Jill."

I laughed. "And so you went and got underground irrigation pipe, carried it to the backyard in the pitch black to avoid the neighbors spotting it, and fell over your own wheelbarrow and broke your leg. Right?"

Mr. Kepple grunted.

"Well, you'd better tell your doctors about this before they spend all your money on brain scans and blood tests. And you'd better—"

He dropped the remote control and took my hand. "Jill, you've got a real interesting case now, right?" he said, demonstrating world-class lack of subtlety.

That silenced me for a moment. "How did you know about that?"

"Read it in the paper," he said, as if reading about

138

current events was an essential part of his routine. I knew better. For Mr. Kepple, newsprint was something on which to wipe his trowel. I sighed. If Mr. Kepple had noticed a report on the case, that meant the article was prominent, probably page one. And it meant the next installment of the story would be all the more appealing when the grieving Mouskavachis planted themselves in the police station lobby. Every newspaper in the Bay Area would dispatch reporters and photographers. TV camera crews would be vying for space. Politicians would demand action, self-appointed advocates would call press conferences. Committees would form to make sure that no city monies expended on the Mouskavachis were being siphoned from more deserving people, places, or things. Every member of the city council would take a position, on both the question of the family and the handling of the case, *my* handling of the case. It'd be press conferences morning and evening and a horde of phone demands in between. Once the Mouskavachis arrived, I'd be lucky to have any time at all to search for Kris's killer.

Since the topic of Mr. Kepple's fellow classmate was where I was headed anyway, I said, "I suppose you know about Hasbrouck Diamond and Leila Sandoval and her eucalyptus tree."

"Oh, yeah. I was taking a class in trees at the time of the arbitration hearing. We spent a whole class discussing how we would trim the eucalypt, if we had to. Of course, no one would have wanted to. Trees that size—it was a *camaldulensis;* they can grow to a hundred and twenty feet in the right conditions—they're hard to trim right to save the shape and keep the relative balance of the branches. And you know, Jill, the danger with eucalyptus branches is—"

"They fall just like that," I said, snapping my fingers. He did a double take, then smiled and patted my hand, as if to say I had done better than he would have expected.

"So no one in your class would have tackled the job?" I asked. "Was that because the job required more training than you had?"

The look of approval faded from his face. "No, Jill. Leila Sandoval's tree was topped. Any moron, any moron without principles, that is, can run a chain saw through a tree. Stoned as he was most of the time, careless as he was even when he was straight, even he could do that."

"Do you mean Cypress?"

"He's the one Leila Sandoval chose to top the tree, Jill. I'd have thought you'd know that."

"Cypress—where is he now?"

"Up north, I heard. But I don't know. I wasn't friendly with him, Jill. He had nothing to offer. He wasn't really interested in gardening. It wasn't just me, Jill, no one wanted to work with him. You could never count on him to do his part. If he was supposed to buy the fertilizer, he forgot. If it was his job to mulch he did it too late, or not at all. The guy was a flake, Jill. Even by Berkeley standards he was a flake."

"He was thrown out of the school, right?"

"And none too soon. He was a hophead, Jill."

There was a term I hadn't heard for years. "Was he dealing?"

"Dealing? I don't know. I didn't get involved in things like that. He wouldn't have asked about that in class. In classes—I had a couple with him—he just wanted to know about growing plants. We all knew what plants he meant. Jill, everybody laughed about him."

"Leila Sandoval must have been able to find out what he was like."

"She called the school for names and recommendations. I know for a fact that no one would have recommended him. He never passed a class."

"And would she have been able to discover his interest in growing marijuana?"

Mr. Kepple's eye opened wide. "Ah, Jill, I see what you're asking. You want to know if she was looking for someone to grow her marijuana, right? It's her land he's got up there near Garberville, right? He's just a tenant farmer, right?" He was all but bouncing up and down on the bed, bouncing his casted leg.

I had assumed that Leila Sandoval had hired a gardener to top her trees and then discovered that he was interested in growing marijuana. It could have been the other way around. Very possibly, Leila Sandoval got word of Cypress's proclivities and that was why she chose him to top her trees and end her poverty.

As he had done to me not five minutes before, I reached over and patted Mr. Kepple's hand in approval.

◆
18
◆

THE departmental meeting room is underneath the jail. At Detectives' Morning Meeting, we all sit around the square formed by the tables in the middle of the room. Then there's no one looking through the windows from the watch commander's office or from the four holding cells that hug the walls. But after Morning Meeting the character of the room changes, as if the room itself took off its jacket and loosened its tie. Sworn officers tap on the watch commander's window, before being motioned in to make reports or give explanations. Patrol officers rush to and from the communications center upstairs, clutching the goldenrod cards on which the calls in are recorded. Officers drag the old wooden chairs together and rest paper cups of vile machine coffee on the table as they swap information.

Sometimes we interview witnesses at the table as I had done this morning with Bev Zagoya. It's an effective technique. A lot of official tan passes by. And holstered guns. And beepers. Through the door the witnesses can see rows of metal file cabinets; they hear officers talking about running names through PIN, through CORPUS, run-

142

ning latents through the new computer in Oakland. It reminds them what their odds are.

I could have brought Leila Sandoval out there. She was sitting in one of the holding cells, a small, old-fashioned school-roomish affair with one wooden chair and the one window overlooking all the activity in the meeting room. But keeping suspects in the holding cells has its own benefits. From inside there the suspects can see the fingers of Big Brother in Blue (or, in our case, tan) but can't hear anything except the dire warnings of their own imaginations.

Leila Sandoval watched it all, as she shifted on the hard chair and shivered in that same T-shirt she had worn on Telegraph Avenue, the one with the sketch of the foot. Despite her sudden and unexpected departure from Garberville, her Kewpie doll makeup was in place—the turquoise eye shadow and the black mascara, the bright pink lipstick and the circles of rouge on her cheeks. Twenty years ago her delicate silky skin must have been like porcelain. Now, even the bright colors couldn't seduce the eye away from the myriad of tiny lines that veiled her face. Her once blond hair was streaked with gray. She looked like a Kewpie doll that had been left in the attic all those years—old, dusty, forgotten.

Had it not been for her muscular shoulders and the scabrous-foot T-shirt, I would have pictured her doing nothing so down to earth as massage: I would have pictured her doing nothing at all, a living carnival prize.

I sat down at the square table where she could see me, and fingered through a folder. The most intimidating-looking papers in it were the standard forms, but Sandoval wouldn't know that. Had she been reading over my shoulder, she would have seen an innocuous-looking note; that was what should have worried her. In it Raksen had said, "Oil on the chaise runners scented with patchouli." Patchouli oil was a favorite in massage.

I let my gaze wash over her as she sat in the holding cell—another technique to soften up a suspect, or get one on edge. Sandoval looked edgy all right, as would any woman in her right mind after she had been picked up sunning herself in the middle of ten acres of marijuana. Did she look as nervous as a murder suspect should, I asked myself, as if there were a reliable scale of blush or twitching quotient. Hallstead, the Humboldt County sheriff, hadn't mentioned Kris Mouskavachi's death to her. It was too soon for word of it to have made the news in Humboldt County. But a neighbor from Berkeley could have called her. If so, she would ask about the murder first thing. If she didn't, I'd wait to see what she revealed. And I'd nail her.

I strode into the holding cell, yanked a chair in behind me, and shut the door.

"You are in a lot of trouble," I said.

Her face quivered. From cold, or fear? About Kris, or something else?

"Possession of one ounce of a controlled substance is a felony."

"I didn't—"

"You were growing ten acres of it up there in Humboldt."

"Not me. I live in Berkeley." Was that relief on her face? Relief about the Berkeley excuse, or at me asking about drugs rather than murder?

I shook my head. "It doesn't matter where you live; you *own* the land on which cannabis is being grown."

"I rent it out."

"Your name is on the deed."

"Yes, but I don't live there. I have a renter. I don't go up there. On the lease it says I can't come onto the property without notifying him first."

I let out a laugh. "Leila, a stipulation like that is an

announcement that you know exactly what's going on in those fields."

The skin around her mouth tightened. "My tenant, he insisted on that; I didn't. I have no idea what goes on up there."

I leaned back, slowly shaking my head. Few attitudes irritated me as much as this righteous air of irresponsibility. Particularly when the speaker was lying. But Sandoval was giving me such a first-rate show of "not me" that the act blurred what it was she was covering up.

I said, "The issue of the land is between you and the Humboldt County sheriff. And, of course, the CAMP authorities." I fingered the file. "Too bad it's up there."

The look of panic on her face told me I didn't have to explain the difference in attitude up there. Her fear of CAMP was the real thing. She took a deep breath, as if to bring herself under control, looked straight at me, and said, "What are you offering?"

I almost laughed again. So much for the helpless featherhead. "There's a big range in how they can handle you. A woman who does massage on Telegraph Avenue is not going to be a sympathetic figure in the Eureka courthouse. You know that."

She nodded, all business now.

"But a woman who has supported the police effort here, she'll have a much better chance of being believed when she testifies about her tenant and his use of her land. A woman who has cooperated in a murder investigation . . ."

She stiffened. The reaction seemed too slight for the first discovery of a murder. But reactions vary.

I chose a tack and said, "You don't seem surprised that there's been a murder." If she'd killed Kris, she'd had since the middle of last night to get accustomed to the idea of him dead. And she'd had the three hours or so since Hallstead picked her up to plan her reactions to these questions. And, it was clear to me already, Leila Sandoval was an accomplished actress.

"I'm stunned. I've known about Kris for a while, but I'm still stunned."

"How'd you find out?"

"A friend called."

"From Berkeley?" That would be a message unit call, one that would be on the friend's phone bill.

She shook her head. "No. A friend up north. Someone called him."

I smiled sardonically, "A series of calls which can't be checked." Before she could comment, I said, "Tell me about Kris Mouskavachi. You brought him over here. Why?"

She sat there, tapping those marmotlike teeth together. "The thing about Kris," she said, thoughtfully, "was that he was on Bev's last expedition. Bev's been worried about this new expedition. And it isn't easy for her living with Has-Bitched. I thought having Kris here would make it easier for her."

I nodded, slowly, at the same rate she had been tapping her teeth. "That's a nice story. Now what is the truth?"

Those wrinkles on her face looked deeper, darker, and lots tighter. She sighed, and said, "Okay. I guess it was naive to expect you to believe I was just interested in making things easier at Has-Bitched's. You probably think I was out to get him. I can understand that. And God knows, I would get him if I could think of a way. But this is different." She leaned forward and looked straight at me, with what I figured was her Earnest Look. "Do you know about Bev's last expedition? Three people died."

I nodded.

"Well, Kris was on that. Kris was convinced that they wouldn't have died if the leader had been competent. I know Bev, and that lack of planning, and the arrogance

146

that made her think that no matter what happened, she could pull things out. When she leads this new expedition, she'll be just as arrogant and just as scattered. The only difference is that there will be more people involved, more people who may die."

"The word on her last expedition is common knowledge."

"No, that's not quite true," she said, reaching a hand toward me as if to touch my arm. Her face was more relaxed now, but there was an urgency to her posture. "Only a little is knowledge. Most of what's known is rumor. You're talking about something that happened halfway around the world, on the side of a mountain, where the climbers are not only cut off from the outside world, but frequently from each other. Accidents are common. Facts vary depending on who you're talking to. So most of what's circulating in the climbing community is conjecture. And Bev's a pro at dealing with that. She may be scattered, but she's also a performer, a salesman. And that arrogance of hers gives her an air of competence." Leila reached out a hand again, again drawing it back at the last moment. "I've seen Bev give lectures and do fund raising. She talks about using computers to determine the number of porters it will take to carry the supplies to base camp, and the number from there to advance base, and from there to Camp One on the mountain, and having the computer factor in the increased amount of grain needed if the weather is ten degrees colder. It sounds like NASA is doing the planning. Businessmen can barely keep themselves from throwing checks at her. Other climbers begin to think the rumors must have been wrong. Bev's the best at this. If no one contradicts her, she'll get her backing, she'll get other climbers—not the best ones, the ones who know better; she'll get the less experienced, the ones with good enough credentials to appeal to the sponsors, the one who won't have a chance if things get desperate up on the mountain. If no one contradicts her, these people will die." Now she did put an "earnest" hand on my arm. "Bev," she said, "is a pro at conning people."

Coming from Leila Sandoval that was quite an endorsement. I was tempted to ask, "A pro at conning Hasbrouck Diamond? Luring him away from you?" But I didn't want her focusing on that, not yet. Instead, I sat watching her. She pulled her hand back. It was shaking. If Leila Sandoval was lying about Bev, it was a great act. I said, "So you brought Kris Mouskavachi here to contradict Bev? At her reception today?"

She nodded. "Kris was on the expedition. He was friends with one of the Sherpas who died. People would believe him."

"But Bev must have known that."

"To her, he was just one of the porters, a little more valuable because he spoke English."

"Bev said they were close friends. She gave him her new wristwatch."

Leila laughed. "Bev *gave* somebody something? Giving is not her style. She figures her presence is gift enough. She gave Kris a wristwatch? Maybe *she* thought they were friends. No, wait, no, Bev's not that thick. Kris's friend was one of the two Sherpas. And Kris blamed her for his friend's death."

I jotted down a note and said, "Then it seems very odd indeed that when Kris suddenly turned up here, that she was pleased to have him come and stay at Diamond's with her."

Now Leila smiled. "She didn't have a choice." She ran her hands down over her thighs in a little self-congratulatory massage. "You know all about my squabbles with Has-Bitched, right?"

I nodded.

"Well, one thing I've learned from them is timing. That story about him thinking my client letting out his emotions was a wounded cougar howling in the hills, that wouldn't have even made the paper if he hadn't made the call in August when there's no other news worth printing. I've had plenty of time to think about that. So when I brought Kris over here, I made sure it was at the right time—when Bev had just left for a month in the Alps. A month was plenty long enough for Kris to ingratiate himself with Has-Bitched."

"Wait! How could you be sure Diamond would take to him?"

She looked surprised. "Everyone likes Kris. You knew him."

"But when you were planning this, before Kris came, you didn't know what he was like."

She pressed her front teeth together.

"Or did you?" I asked. "You did, right? You had to know that Kris could charm Diamond. How did you know what Kris was like?"

"Bev told me."

"Bev, to whom Kris was just another porter? Come on." I waited, and when she didn't reply, said, "Our deal here is dependent on your giving me the truth. Don't put me in the position of telling Humboldt you lied to me."

In the meeting room what sounded like a battalion of feet trod across the floor. Morning Watch (7:00 A.M.–3:00 P.M.) was winding down. Patrol officers had come in, preparing to write up reports, pass on the word of suspicious cars parked off Sacramento Avenue, of crazies on the Avenue to the Evening Watch guys who'd be rolling soon.

Leila tapped her teeth ever more slowly. Finally, she said, "I know Kris's cousin."

I waited till she said his name. The cousin, of course, was Cypress. Cypress, who looked like Kris. I found myself tapping my pencil in rhythm with her tapping

149

teeth. "You'd better tell me about this from the beginning."

"The beginning with Cypress?"

"Wherever the beginning is."

She leaned back in the spare wooden chair and pulled her ankle up onto her knee. She looked like the post-massage version of the nervous woman who'd answered my initial question. "Well, I guess the beginning was with Has-Bitched and the tree. I never thought he would actually be able to force me to top my tree. I mean, this *is* Berkeley, for heaven's sake; trees do have rights. His winning that ruling took me completely by surprise. There was no recourse, no way to get even with that bastard. So I did the best thing I could think of. Under the law I was the one who chose the tree trimmer. Has-Bitched had to concur, but I chose. So I checked around and found the most irresponsible, least qualified tree trimmer and told him to charge Has-Bitched a fortune. I figured he'd do a lousy job, which he did, and the tree would be an eyesore from Has-Bitched's deck, which I've been told it is."

"But it's your tree!" I exclaimed. I did note that Diamond's assessment of the situation concurred with Sandoval's story.

Leila laughed. "Eucalypts are hardy. Besides, once a tree is topped, we're not talking aesthetics anymore. And, since I'm giving you the truth, I don't care a hang about trees. The only benefit of those eucalypts is that they save me from having to see Has-Bitched parading around in his baggy birthday suit."

I looked through the window, watching as Murakawa strolled across the meeting room, dark hair disheveled, a disarming smile on his face, not unlike Kris Mouskavachi's had been. "Since we are dealing with the *whole* truth here, when did you get the idea of having Cypress gouge out the crotch of the tree and add the bacteria?"

It's odd what suspects balk at admitting, often the

least incriminating facts, often facts that have nothing to do with the case. I wouldn't have expected Leila to freeze on this one, but she did. She shook her head slowly and said, "I can't say what Cypress did. I didn't watch him on the tree. But I do know bacteria spread from tree to tree, and it's almost impossible to keep them out of stagnant water."

"And you do know that Diamond is liable for any expense caused by the tree topping."

She almost smiled, caught herself, then nodded.

"And after this affair," I said, "you signed a rental agreement with this man whom you knew to be probably the most unreliable gardener in Berkeley. You gave him control of your land in Humboldt, and agreed to stay off the property so you wouldn't see what he was doing. *And* he paid not a cent of rent for a year. That's quite a hefty thank-you. What was it all for?"

"For Kris. For the chance to warn the people who would otherwise be climbing with Bev."

I shook my head. "The truth!"

Her face colored just slightly. "That is the truth, or part of it," she added with a tentative smile. "Bev is a danger. But okay, it wasn't all altruism on my part. The thousand dollars for travel was a lot of money, and money isn't something I have much of. But I was pissed off at Bev. After all she was my friend originally, and then when Has-Bitched offered her a free room, she acted like we'd never been friends at all. It appealed to me to do something decent—warn people—and to get her at the same time."

"And to get Hasbrouck Diamond, your former lover?"

She shut her eyes and didn't move. Slowly she shook her head and her eyes opened. "The mistake of my life." All she had said before may have been part of her act. Every reaction may have been fake. But this, I was willing

151

to bet, was bedrock truth. "Climbers talk about the Big Mistake. You can guess what that is."

From Bev's lecture, I knew what that was. Bev had also referred to it as the Last Step.

"Well, that dalliance with Hasbrouck Diamond was my Big Mistake. Hasbrouck turned my life upside down. Then he shook me out." She paused, watching me for reaction.

I had the feeling she'd told this story often enough before to know when to stop and gather in offerings of sympathy, that for her even the truth became part of the act. And the act became the truth. It made her almost impossible to read. I nodded for her to go on.

"And as if that wasn't enough, then he started on me about my house, and how shabby it was. As if he didn't know how little money I had, and why. And then his friends parked in front of my driveway—"

"And so, to get back to your bringing Kris over here to expose Bev," I said, to cut into this rehash of the feud, "it appealed to you to make a mockery of Bev's presentation, and particularly so because Hasbrouck Diamond had set it up, in his own house?"

Leila couldn't control the smile. It was a big infectious grin. "The thought did occur to me. I kind of hoped he'd have invited a couple of those Hollywood types he tries to impress."

"And the bees?"

"The bees," she said, clearly delighted. "A wonderful touch, don't you think? See, for Has-Bitched having Bev was like owning the prize pig. And it would have been wonderful to see that pig stumble out all covered in shit."

"Particularly when it was that pig he left you for?"

I took her quick intake of breath for a yes, and said, "But, of course, none of that would have happened."

"Why not?" she demanded in a small, tight voice.

I repeated what Bev Zagoya had told me. "Because Kris told Diamond that you paid his way here."

"Kris wouldn't have!"

"And he canceled the order for the bees."

Leila's face flushed, the lines in it maroon, and her eyes opened so wide that the whites were visible all the way around. "How could he . . . ? He knew about Bev. He was so grateful to get out of Kathmandu, so very grateful to make use of my money, so . . . The fucking little opportunist!"

"And so," I prodded, "Diamond got you again, right?"

But she didn't answer. She just stared.

"And then you got Kris." Before she could regroup, I said, "I need the key to your house."

Now she did look up. Her panicked expression was no put-on. "Why? I don't have to—"

"I need your house key. I can get a search warrant. That'll just take longer. It'll just make me angrier. It'll make me inclined to call Humboldt and give them my theory: A woman needs money. She has ten acres of land in the country. She might be able to sell it, but not for a great deal, and probably not quickly. She couldn't rent it for much unless she could put a decent house on it, which she can't afford to do. So what is the one thing for which she could lease ten acres that would bring the kind of money she needs? My theory, Leila, is that Cypress didn't happen along and seduce you into law breaking; you called the gardening school and discovered that a student had been thrown out of their classes, realized why, and made him an offer, with the tree trimming as a cover."

"That's ridiculous!" she said, her voice shaking. "It's all speculation. You've got no proof," she said, in those words giving me all the proof I needed.

"The skill of the police is finding proof. But, as I said, this is only a theory I am considering passing on to the

153

Humboldt sheriff. Perhaps, if I have your key and am involved in my own investigation, the Humboldt sheriff will see your case differently than I might have."

She continued to stare. Then her breath came faster, she opened her mouth, and spit out one word. "Lawyer."

"Leila, Kris Mouskavachi is dead, murdered!"

She froze.

"Someone," I said, staring at her, "pushed the chaise Kris was sleeping on off the end of Hasbrouck Diamond's deck. And Leila, the runners of that chaise were oiled with patchouli oil."

Slowly, she reached into her pocket. With a shaking hand she held out the key to me. She was hiding something in her house, something she was gambling I wouldn't find. And that something was not patchouli oil.

19

I GOT a statement of whereabouts from Leila Sandoval for the times of the eucalyptus attack and Kris's death. She had been on the Avenue, doing feet, when the branch fell, she said, and up in Humboldt at a party with Cypress last night. Both alibis could be checked. Both could be faked. Neither meant anything.

Hallstead, the Humboldt County sheriff's deputy who had brought Sandoval down here, was talking about the new drug laws and conspiracy. There was no way Sandoval would be traveling outside of custody for a while.

Whereas Bev Zagoya could be going anywhere any moment if I didn't get her now. I thought about that expensive new Swiss watch that she said she had given Kris Mouskavachi, and what that interchange told me. Bev Zagoya had a lot to explain.

I signed out a patrol car and drove back past the few browsers who braved the thickening fog on Telegraph.

At Diamond's house the fog was dense. And no one was home. I looked over toward San Francisco. By now the entire city was hidden and only the top of Treasure Island was still poking through the gray ooze.

I called into the dispatcher and left word for Hallstead to meet me to search Leila Sandoval's house. And find whatever it was she had been so anxious to keep hidden. Then I wandered back down onto Hasbrouck Diamond's deck and looked at the spot where the eucalyptus branch had scraped Diamond. An oval of sun surrounded it. I could picture Diamond sitting there, skinny legs thrust out, pleated tan skin of his torso shining in that island of hot sun surrounded by the shade from Leila Sandoval's trees.

I walked down to the far end. The gate was shut now. I looked over the edge of the deck. A jolt of dizziness fogged my head and queasiness filled my stomach. I held my gaze. Both those things would pass. And if they didn't I'd just go on looking down and feeling lousy. The chaise that Kris had been on was gone, of course. Raksen would be savoring fibers and paint chips from it. He'd be doing ever more subtle tests on the patchouli oil from the runners. By now there was little to suggest to the unknowing that a boy had died down below here. Weeds and vines and scrub brush covered the rock where Kris had hit. I wondered how familiar Bev Zagoya was with that rock. Could she have figured that was where Kris would land? Diamond and Leila would have known, of course, but Bev's bedroom window was closest to that spot.

The dizziness and queasiness eased up. I stepped back, briefly savoring my small victory. I tried to picture Kris asleep on his chaise. But it wasn't so easy as imagining Hasbrouck Diamond. Kris Mouskavachi covered head to toe with a sleeping bag—why didn't that seem right? Kris himself told me he slept out there. From his description of his life with his parents in Kathmandu, he would hardly have been offended by the ambience on Hasbrouck Diamond's deck. For anyone accustomed to sleeping out,

156

this deck was elegance. Gus, the street person who'd taken up residence in Howard's shed, would have been in heaven, at least in the warm weather. In winter it would have been another story. But Kris had grown up in Nepal, he wouldn't have been bothered by the prospect of cold. I tried to picture Gus here on that chaise. But that wasn't right either. Gus was too dirty, too disheveled, too much a street person for Hasbrouck Diamond to allow on his fine deck. But Kris, in his new rugby shirt and still clean running shoes, why couldn't I picture him here?

"Jill!" It was Howard, calling from the archway.

Leaving my speculation unanswered, I walked across the deck. "Couldn't resist coming here, huh?" I said.

"Hallstead has to have a liaison in Substance Abuse. Someone has to give up his Saturday afternoon"—he lowered his voice—"when he could be doing lots better things with the woman of his choice, if she were around."

I grinned. "Had nothing to do with the fact that you are the only guy on the force who hasn't been to the crime scene, huh? Never mind, I like your explanation better."

Hallstead was waiting on the sidewalk, under the paperbark tree. "For years I kept hearing the old Mark Twain saying, 'The coldest winter I ever spent—'"

"'Was one summer in San Francisco,'" Howard and I chimed in as we headed up the bulging, broken sidewalk to Leila Sandoval's door.

It looked, if anything, even worse than it had two days before. The weeds and shrubs and vines that gathered around every orifice varied in shade from sallow green to downright brown. The caramel-colored goo that coated the cracks looked much darker than I recalled, much darker than the faded paint it had been intended to match. The brown wooden door was scuffed and scraped and its foot-square stained-glass window had three diagonal cracks.

I opened the door and walked in. I had expected the

cottage to be stuffy, which it was. I had also assumed it would be cool. But the heat from the last few days hung on in here.

Hallstead groaned. "Wouldn't you think someone with windows that run the full west side of their house would have the sense to pull the drapes?"

"Or have drapes," I added. Somehow that didn't surprise me. The tiny house was exactly what I would have pictured for Leila Sandoval. On the right, a small bedroom crowded by the street. To the left was a narrow kitchen with a counter dividing it from the main room that filled the rest of the house.

Hallstead had already finished with the kitchen when I started. "Nothing there, believe me," he grumbled. "Nothing but seeds and dried beans and rice."

Still, I checked every drawer and cabinet and the refrigerator. Hallstead had missed the tofu and the Japanese eggplant.

The main room that faced the deck was divided into living room and massage studio. The living room section (the end farthest from Hasbrouck Diamond's) was about twelve by sixteen with a stone fireplace, a tweed couch, a couple of bucket chairs, and a splattering of magazines, newspapers, a few sweaters and T-shirts, and a variety of sandals, running shoes, and clogs sprinkled like black pepper over a salad.

In contrast the massage area was so tidy it could have been sterile. There was nothing in that half of the room but the massage table, a pile of clean and folded sheets, a wicker basket for the used sheets. And a bookcase with ten bottles of massage oil—almond, sandalwood, and eight other scents. But not patchouli. I was surprised. I would have expected to find patchouli in a massage studio. Its absence was more damning than its presence would have been, unless, of course, that oil could have been differentiated from all other bottles of patchouli and then matched to the oil on the chaise runners. I took samples of the other oils for Raksen, reminding myself as I did so to go back to the kitchen and take samples of the oil there. And not to forget the garage. And to have Raksen up here to see if there was any trace left of patchouli oil flushed down the toilet, or poured down the sink or over her deck railing. A wise murderer would have dumped an incriminating bottle in the Bay. But Leila's actions in the last twenty-four hours did not bespeak wisdom and forethought.

One thing both sections of the living room had in common—there was no place to hide anything.

After the brightness by the deck windows, Leila Sandoval's bedroom seemed cavelike. It had only one small window that opened onto Panoramic and admitted no more light than the tiny and none too clean window in my office. The shade was up, but vines covered about half the surface. This was definitely the back-alley room of the house. Definitely a hiding place of choice. A double-bed mattress lay on the floor (where it would be firmer, I guessed). The bed was unmade. A bedside table held the usual things, and a collection of books about feet and foot massage; also, I found to my surprise, a number on anatomy. The dresser contained nothing unexpected. One closet was jammed with Leila's clothes. I searched through, T-shirt by T-shirt, sweatpants by sweatpants. If she had her crucial secret in here, it was too small or subtle for me.

But when I opened the other closet I found the answer to my question on Diamond's deck. I called to Howard.

"Look at this," I said. The closet held carefully spaced hangers holding ten pairs of slacks, with labels from Cable Car Clothiers; about the same number of shirts, some striped, some dress; five rugby shirts; a sweatshirt that still had a fifty-dollar price tag on it, with sweatpants to match; and another set in a different color. There were running shoes, hiking shoes, boots, and sandals.

Howard whistled. "Whoever lives here spends a whole lot more on his body than I do."

"These are Kris Mouskavachi's clothes. I recognize the rugby shirt and running shoes he had on yesterday."

Howard whistled again. Hallstead poked his head in. "What's this?" he demanded. "You guys trying out for the Seven Dwarfs?" He looked again at Howard's long frame and added, "In a whistle-while-you-work sense."

Howard said, "Jill's murder victim arrived from Kathmandu six weeks ago with barely a rupee, and now he's got a couple of thousand dollars of clothes."

Hallstead nodded knowingly. In Humboldt, with the marijuana farm set, sudden wealth has no surprise.

"I doubt Kris was in drugs," I said, slowly. "Unless he was a onetime courier, there's no way he would have come into so much money so soon."

"Then where did he get his young-man-around-town wardrobe?" Howard asked.

I sighed. "Hasbrouck Diamond would be the best guess, except that then these clothes would have been at his house. Kris was sleeping on his deck. Diamond may have known Leila brought Kris to this country, but until today Leila didn't know that he knew. And neither of them would have been so aboveboard about it as to allow Kris to go traipsing back and forth from house to house every morning as he dressed."

That picture apparently pleased Hallstead, who settled himself on the unmade bed and laughed. Howard leaned back against the wall next to the window and ran his thumb and first finger down his lantern chin, thinking. "But with that wardrobe here in her house, Sandoval would have kept a hold on Mouskavachi while he was living with the enemy."

I saluted him. Howard, the department sting expert,

was in his element here. The clothes had to be Leila's well-guarded secret. "A hold that made him do what?"

Howard shook his head.

I started to shut the closet door and stood swinging it from hand to hand, trying to formulate just what was bothering me. "Okay, guys," I said, "give me the benefit of your masculine expertise."

Howard grinned. Pontificating on life with the Y-chromosome was another area he claimed as his own.

I went on. "Now you can picture the nineteen-year-old who arranged this closet," I said, pulling the door back open.

"I can't," Hallstead said. "My wife would think she'd died and gone to heaven if our son hung up his clothes like that."

"Probably about three kids in the entire state would be this fussy about their clothes," I said. "And, unless Kris was lying about his parents, he didn't inherit neatness. So, guys, what we've got here is the real Kris Mouskavachi. This well-dressed kid was a guest next door, in a luxurious house with two extra bedrooms. Can you imagine him choosing to forego the luxury of the better of those bedrooms so he could sleep on the deck in a sleeping bag?"

They both laughed. It was Hallstead who said, "And get up all wrinkled?"

"So," Howard asked, "why was he out there?"

"And why were his clothes over here? So he could keep pretending to Diamond that he was just an earnest kid from Nepal here to help his friend Bev. When I saw him Friday at Diamond's he was wearing the same rugby shirt and jeans he was wearing yesterday. They weren't fresh Friday. So maybe for Diamond's viewing he wore only a couple of shirts, only what he could justify having and still maintain his image."

"For where your treasure is, there will your heart be

161

also," Hallstead pronounced. "Matthew six, twenty-one," he added. "I aim to bring some authority to this investigation."

Howard shook his head and glanced back at the closet. "So, with all this, Leila Sandoval knew just what a good actor Kris was. And how much he liked luxury."

"She hasn't had her head between someone's toes all these years. And she's no slouch when it comes to putting on a show herself," I said. "She was on to Kris. She knew he was an opportunist; she just didn't realize how far he'd go. Still, once she gave him the clothes, she would have realized that Kris had made what use of her he could. Because she didn't have much, he'd already sucked her dry. Why should he remain loyal to her when he could align himself with Diamond?"

"And with Bev Zagoya?" Howard said. "And with the money men who sponsored her new expedition?"

I leaned back against the wall, staring out the small vine-covered window. "Then that would mean Kris planned to support Bev in today's presentation. That fits with Kris canceling the bees. And that would mean there would be nothing unusual happening, nothing newsworthy, nothing to bring out all those reporters who rushed over there when they heard about Kris's death."

"So, conversely," Howard said, "if there was something newsworthy, it would have been something a lot more serious than the bees. Something like Kris planning to undermine Bev and come out with some sort of revelation about the deaths on the previous climbs."

I nodded. "Umm. Then the question is, why would he have done that? Leila would be delighted, of course. It would be her ultimate revenge on Diamond. It would explain the clothes here, and why Leila was anxious for me not to see them and find out there was one final change of loyalties she hadn't told me about. But what would be in it for Kris?"

Hallstead was sitting shaking his head.

But Howard pushed off the wall and said, "What would Kris want? Tell me about him."

"His goal was to be CEO of some Pacific Rim international business."

"So maybe he was going to ingratiate himself with the business people who would *not* be wasting money on Bev's next expedition."

"And," I said, "Kris loved attention. Well, he'd get plenty of that. Whatever news coverage this affair got, it would have pictured Kris unmasking an incompetent, Kris saving lives and money."

"Not a bad way to start out in business school."

A flash of red and yellow passed the window. "Howard," I said excitedly, "Leila worked in public relations. She knows who to call, what to say, how to get news coverage. That, Howard, is what was still left for Kris to suck out of Leila. And— Omigod, that's Bev Zagoya."

"Where?"

"On Panoramic. Running. *Up* Panoramic." I raced out the door, down the hill, unlocked the patrol car door, and started the engine. The patrol car has a big engine; it's useless on a road like this. There's no way to go above twenty on the straightaway, or ten on the cutbacks. Once I rounded the corner I could see Zagoya in the distance, taking the next curve to the right and moving out of sight. I stepped on the gas and spotted her again. She was wearing that yellow T-shirt and red shorts, and a purple fanny pack bounced on her pelvis. As I neared her I could see the bulge of the oblong contents in the pack. I blew the horn.

She turned, spotted the car, looked at me with an expression of shock and anger she might have shown Kris Mouskavachi when she first came upon him on Diamond's deck, and ran faster.

I stepped on the gas. She rounded the corner. I had to slow to five mph to get by a Mercedes parked on the curve. And when I came to the short straightaway Bev Zagoya was nowhere in sight.

I didn't spot her till I came to the fire trail that ended at Panoramic. Then I saw her a hundred yards or so in the distance. She was running easily on the dirt track. A lot more easily than I would. More easily than she would have if there hadn't been a pole blocking auto access to the trail.

She was almost out of sight when she glanced around. She was smiling. She thought she was safe from me.

She was wrong.

20

THE good news was that as I watched Bev Zagoya disappear at the top of the hill and around the corner onto the fire trail, I was ninety-five percent sure where she was going—particularly when I noted her purple fanny pack. Why would she be wearing a pack? What could she need enough to carry the extra weight during a run? Not a sweatshirt; the pack was too small. Money she'd carry in a shoe purse; tissues she'd tuck in her belt. The thing she'd carry would be those sticky, rubber rock-climbing shoes. Climbing shoes fit like foot bindings. They're not shoes to walk in, much less run in. There was only one climbing place the trail led to: Grizzly Peak Rock, a forty-foot-high face hidden high in the Berkeley Hills.

The bad news was that Grizzly Peak Rock was two miles away, and actually in Oakland rather than Berkeley. I would have to spend more time calling the dispatcher and having him notify Oakland.

But the best news was that there was a way for me to get there without running along the fire trail after Bev Zagoya and demonstrating that I was in nowhere near as good shape as she. I could drive down Panoramic, behind campus, up Centennial Road, and back this way on Grizzly Peak Road, and be plunked coolly atop the rock waiting when she trotted up panting and sweaty. *If* I could get there in less than the ten minutes or so she would need. Any later and she'd spot me before I could get in position to take her by surprise. I yanked the wheel all the way to the right, turned around, and headed down Panoramic.

Howard was just coming out of Leila Sandoval's house when I came abreast it. "Bev Zagoya's heading for Grizzly Peak Rock. I'll be waiting for her at the top."

"You need back-up?" he said, shifting his stance in readiness to move around the car and climb in.

"Be at the far end of the fire trail. Zagoya won't make it to the rock for fifteen minutes. If she keeps going—there's no reason why she should—it would be twenty minutes before she'd get to the trail's end. You've got time to drop Hallstead near the station."

He nodded.

I stepped on the gas, driving down Panoramic as fast as I dared between the parked cars, squealing the tires on the sharp cutbacks. I put on the pulsers as I turned the corner off Panoramic and into the campus fraternity area. Bev had a run of about a mile and a half. My drive would be at least twice that, and through one of the most crowded areas in town. As I neared the corner, four students sauntered into the crosswalk, all talking, hands waving in emphasis. For all the notice they took of traffic, they might have been sitting around a table in a cafe; they didn't even react to the pulser lights. I flicked on the siren. They leapt back as one, and scowled. I hung a right.

I turned off the siren long enough to call the dispatcher. He'd notify Oakland and the Day Watch commander. Then I turned it back on to get through the campus roads. My fingers tightened on the steering wheel. The wail of the siren blotted out everything else; it turned the car into a capsule. Just me and the car and the chase. I loved it. I raced along the sharply curving road, up the hillside, between the redwoods and eucalypts that crowded the road. On the curves, I pressed harder on the gas and leaned into the turns. The tires squealed. The staccato bursts from the radio goaded me on, like the whip of a jockey's crop.

I made it to the parking lot by the rockface in eight minutes. There were no other cars. It was late in the day for rock climbing.

The rockface stands just in front of the hillside beneath the parking area, the way a thumbnail is in front of an upturned thumb. The parking area is on top. Most climbers start there, walk over the tip of the thumb, and climb down the nail. But looking up from the fire trail, there is no suggestion that a road, much less a parking turnout, is there at all.

The afternoon wind iced the sweat on my face and back. I raced across the dirt lot and clambered down the hillside (from the tip of the thumb down behind the nail) and peered over the edge of the rock. I couldn't see all the way to the underbrush below the rock. But Bev Zagoya was not on the face. No one was. Only a couple of abandoned ropes hung down it from hooks that had been pounded into the top of the rock. I looked down the fire trail to my left. No sign of Bev. Could I have been wrong about her heading here? Could that bulge in her pack have been a water bottle, or a couple of oranges? Could she be sprawled on the wooden bench back along the fire trail, gazing out over the tops of the pines and eucalypts, past the carillon tower on campus, watching the fog flow in from the ocean?

Staring down at the underbrush, it occurred to me that every single person I'd heard mention climbing this rock face had come at it from the top. Was the ground down below too uncertain to try? Was the—I laughed silently. I was viewing that problem from the wrong end. The underbrush wasn't the issue. No one worried whether it was too thick or the ground beneath it too treacherous. It wasn't that the underbrush was the minus, it was that the parking lot at the top was the plus.

I glanced back to the left, and sighed. In the distance were the yellow shirt and red shorts. I moved back behind the shield of the rock to wait. The dirt had a dank smell. The rock was cold and slippery from the fog; it was hard to believe that just yesterday it had been ninety degrees here. After one night of fog it was like the sun had never shone at all. I remembered Bev this morning, in her shorts and sleeveless top, oblivious to the cold as she stood on the roof hosing down the window boxes.

Moving forward inch by inch, I peered cautiously over the edge of the rock face. My stomach lurched. It was forty feet, straight down. I closed my eyes and swallowed hard, then forced myself to look again. Bev Zagoya was at the bottom of the rock changing shoes.

I waited, thinking how much easier this would be if I didn't need answers to key questions. But I did, and I needed to pose them here, on her turf, where a woman who had conquered the Himalaya would feel in control. Where she wouldn't be calling for a lawyer before she spoke.

When I glanced down again, she was on the face maybe ten feet up. Although to me the face looked as smooth as the wall of a three-story building, she was finding handholds and toeholds and moving up with the speed of someone climbing stairs.

I moved back, trying to hear the sound of Bev's rubber-coated shoes, or the scrape of short fingernails in the fingerjams. I thought of Bev Zagoya and that hose on the roof, and the wet crotches in Leila Sandoval's eucalypts. And of the Swiss watch. I thought of Bev Zagoya living in a borrowed room because she couldn't afford her own place. I thought of the years she had devoted to learning to climb, improving her technique, her endurance, running in the heat and the cold and the rain. The years it had taken her to be among the best. And the years she had not spent studying economics, or business administration, or dentistry, or anything that could provide her with a living.

Her dark hair was visible over the rim. I waited one more moment, until she hoisted herself onto the top of the rock, then I pulled myself up beside her and said, "If you couldn't climb anymore, what would you do?"

Her shocked expression could have been the result of seeing me pop up here. For someone else it would have been. But for Bev a rockface would be as natural a place to come across anyone as a bus stop. Like it had been yesterday on Indian Rock, her face was tight with anger, but now there was fear there, too.

"Your whole adult life has been built around climbing. How would you live without it?"

She inched back farther in on the rock. "I could get a job. I have connections."

"I don't mean just financially, I mean what would your life be like as a *former* climber, a woman who *used* to be a mountaineer?"

Despite the cold air, sweat was running down her forehead, and beaded above the hairs on her eyebrows.

"To know it's over," I insisted. "That you'll never stand on another mountaintop again. To have your life be ordinary?" To rip through the curtain of Berkeley syndrome and find the wall behind it more blank and gray and endless than you'd allowed yourself to fear? To not only see the pasture fence but be tethered to it?

"I'll worry about that when the time comes."

I nodded. "That doesn't sound like the organized person who plans her expeditions with a computer."

Her eyebrows lowered, the beads of sweat began to

run down over the hairs. "Some things you have to think about now, some there's no point in worrying about."

"Like when you've already negotiated for the food on an expedition and started out, and then you realize there may not be enough, and you may end up taking a shorter more dangerous route because you haven't got enough food to go the safe way?"

She glared. "Who are you to tell me how to run an expedition?"

I shifted my legs so I could face her. "Oh, no, Bev, this isn't my conclusion, this is Kris's. This is what Kris Mouskavachi would have been saying to those potential investors and all those reporters today, isn't it? He would have been standing in the middle of Hasbrouck Diamond's living room right now telling the filmmakers and the money men that you didn't buy enough food for your last expedition, that you were too arrogant to admit your mistake, and that three people died."

Angrily, she yanked off a climbing shoe, and stared at it. She sat as still, as granitelike as Grizzly Peak Rock. I had expected her to deny the charge, but her silence told me she was jettisoning that defense and deciding what she had left in good enough condition to use. Before she could call up her second line of defense, I said, "You told me Kris was your friend. But he came here to expose you."

She pulled off the other shoe, slapped the two down beside her and said, "What did you expect me to say? Sure I knew about Kris. And I knew what story he'd be spouting. But that's hardly the type of thing you tell a homicide detective. It wouldn't have made me look good, would it?"

I almost laughed. They're usually not that honest, or was it arrogant? "Kris was poised to destroy your career, the career you've spent your entire adult life nurturing."

"Is that what you think? Amateurs!" she snapped, apparently forgetting that my status was way below that.

170

"That just shows you how little you know about mountaineering." She unzipped the fanny pack and pulled out her running shoes. She poked a foot into one and began tightening the laces, catching each section with her forefingers and yanking it taut. "Kris couldn't have done me any harm. What he was spouting was old stuff. Who was going to believe him, a hippie porter?"

"All those reporters outside the house this morning, they figured his death was important enough to come out before dawn. The reason they knew about him is that they had been prepared to be there this afternoon for his announcement."

"I don't care what those people think. I'm a climber, not a TV star." She pulled on the other shoe and slowly began to pull the lace. "Well, okay, so maybe it's not that black and white. Maybe the story would get a mention on some late-night local newscast. But insiders in the climbing world have heard it before, and they've heard my explanation. Look, people die all the time in the Himalaya."

"That may be how climbers see it." A gust ruffled the leaves of the live oaks and eucalyptus beside the rock. It chilled my arms and brought out goose bumps on Bev's. But she didn't seem to notice. "Financial backers," I insisted, "are not likely to be so sanguine about death."

"Backers," she snapped. "I've already got backers. I've got equipment, medical supplies, my airfare covered. And, the promise of ten percent of the film money; I can get a loan off that. Brouck's got a check for my share waiting for me right now. The rest of the backers will get on board. All they care about is the hook. They'd put their money behind the first California expedition on Everest led by a woman if the climbing party were Snow White and the Seven Dwarfs."

"Not if all the dwarfs were likely to die."

She smacked the pack down on the rock. "Backers

171

don't care about that. If they get their shots of me standing on the top in their parka, they won't give a damn about anything else. They're not writing a book, they're looking for a photo opportunity for their gear. Like those posters in the living room. They're going to sell them in stores at campuses all over the country. The kids who buy them aren't going to ask what went on before the photographer pushed the button, or after."

A gust of wind flapped Bev's T-shirt. She didn't shiver, its effect on her was all mental. I could almost see her gears moving as she pulled herself back into control. To me, she said, "To tell you the truth, Kris was a pain in the ass. He was going to create a wrinkle in the cloth of the preparations for this expedition, but he was not going to rip the cloth apart. Mountaineering just isn't like that. You're an outsider, like Brouck; you think that what climbing's about is a great adventure story, with lots of danger, and maybe a tragedy, but with basically a happy ending. That's not it. Mountaineering is a very individual thing. And what it's all about is getting to the top. That's all."

"And the hose on the roof, in position to keep the crotches of Leila Sandoval's eucalyptus trees wet? What was that all about?"

Her eyes opened wide. "Why would you think I—"

"Because Leila's house is on the other side of the tree. Even if she held a hose out the window and squirted the water up week after week without anyone ever noticing, she couldn't have hit the crotch of that branch. It's on the far side from her house. But with the hose on the roof, it would be nothing for you."

"That's ridiculous."

"How soon did you realize there was no way to keep Kris from exposing you? When you first saw him at Diamond's house? No that wouldn't be it, would it? Then

172

you still had hope. Otherwise you wouldn't have given him your watch. Or was that watch a gift?"

"Blackmail," she muttered.

"And all those clothes?"

She stared at me. "I didn't buy him *clothes*. Christ, he was better dressed than I am."

"He had a couple of thousand dollars worth of new things," I insisted.

Bev pressed her whitened fingertips into the rock. "Maybe he did, but he didn't get them from me. I couldn't afford a couple of thousand dollars of anything. And if I had the money, I wouldn't submit to that kind of blackmail. If I did it would be an admission of guilt."

"Easy to say now."

"What do you take me for? I've bargained with the best of them. And the worst. I'd been on a climb with Kris Mouskavachi. I knew what he was."

"You knew nothing short of death would stop him."

Bev dragged her fingers slowly, angrily across the rock. They left trails of chalk. Furiously she said, "Don't you think if I'd pushed Kris off the deck, I would have taken my watch off his wrist first?"

"If you could."

"Look, alive Kris was going to be a pain in the ass, I'll admit it, a big one. But I could have handled that. He was smart, and charming, but he didn't know the ropes like I did. He wasn't an insider. Maybe he would have ruined this expedition, but there would have been others. I'm twenty-eight-years old. I could climb for another fifteen years." She released the rock and stared down at her chalky, callused fingers. Suddenly that lowering brow of hers seemed not so much an indication of anger as grief. "You're not a climber. You don't know the way things are between the real climbers, the insiders. Whoever killed Kris Mouskavachi killed this expedition. No matter who killed him, his death is going to be connected to me. A

173

death on a mountain is ordinary stuff, but a murder is not. The story of Kris flying off a deck in Berkeley is going to get a lot of attention, for a long time. It'll be a notorious legend in the climbing world. And it will destroy me."

She gazed down at her hands, like someone in a trance. The fingers looked stiff, gnarled, white, arthritic, like they might after years of forced inactivity.

She shook her head sharply, turned to me and said, "Kris Mouskavachi being murdered is the worst thing that could have happened to me. Now nothing matters." She spun around, grabbed one of the abandoned ropes, and before I could move she bounced over the edge, pushed off, bounced three more times to the bottom and raced out through the underbrush.

21

I STARED down the face of the rock after her. My stomach jumped. It took me a split second to call up and discard every excuse I could muster to avoid going down that forty-foot drop. I had been to a few climbing lectures and read a couple of books. I understood the *theory* of rappelling down a wall. And the dangers. My throat tightened, my heart thudded. Suddenly my hands were so sweaty I felt sure I'd never hold onto the rope. But there was no escape. I couldn't give in to this fear, not and go on being a cop. Not and go on *being*.

I grabbed the rope, ran it over my shoulder, down across my back, and back toward my navel, and lowered myself over the edge. I didn't bounce like Bev had, I walked down, sliding the rope between my hands. The skin on my palms burned. On my back the rope dragged my shirt up and scraped the bared flesh. The world narrowed to the dull rockface and the thick sound of my breath. I never looked down. And when my foot hit dirt, I almost fell back from surprise.

I followed the path Bev had made. When I reached the fire trail she was almost out of sight. I jogged along the path, slowly catching my breath and getting into a sort of rhythm. I didn't need to catch her (a good thing). I just needed to keep her in sight. To my right the slope dropped off sharply. Gusts of wind rattled the live oak leaves and the eucalypts.

I thought about Leila Sandoval and the pleasure she would have gotten if Kris had made his announcement. And what Bev had said, that the backers who would provide the supplies for the actual expedition didn't care what happened to the climbers on a mountain, that they only wanted the still photos of their gear on top. And about Bev's destroyed career. The truth had been a long time coming, but now I felt sure I had it. I thought about how far ahead Bev Zagoya was getting, how strong her legs were, how strong her arms were.

By the time I reached Hasbrouck Diamond's deck it was all clear in my mind. But by then Bev Zagoya was gone. Only Hasbrouck Diamond was there, standing peering at his feet. "If you're looking for Bev," he said, "she left."

I was panting too hard to speak.

"She needed my check, from the film people. She grabbed it and took off, without so much as a . . ." He was staring at me with an expression of such bewilderment and fear that I almost felt sorry for him.

I remembered the chaise lounge as it had been early this morning, in the brush below. And yesterday as it stood on the deck no more than ten feet from where we were now. I couldn't picture Bev Zagoya's chalky white fingers oiling the runners. I shook my head. "Not her," I gasped. "It's you I'm looking for. You killed Kris. You have . . . the right . . . to remain silent. You . . ."

For a moment Diamond didn't react. Then he spun and ran for the far end of the deck where Kris had gone over. He flung open the gate and grabbed the rappel rope that hung there. Gasping, I ran after him. He poised a foot at the edge of the deck and braced to pivot out. I caught the railing with one hand and with the other grabbed his arm and swung him back toward me. He pulled away. Bracing my feet I let go of the railing, took hold of his shoulder, and slammed him onto the deck.

I'd made myself rappel down a wall once today. I was damned if I was going to do it twice.

22

SATURDAY night, my last night at The Palace. I had intended to spend it with Howard, lounging in the hot tub, gazing out through the nonfog picture window at the string of lights on the Bay Bridge as they twinkled smudgily through the real fog outside. I'd planned to drink the bottle of champagne we'd saved, snuggle down in the hot water, and listen to the deep, shivery breaths of the foghorns.

Instead, I devoted the evening to Hasbrouck Diamond. When I took his first statement, about the eucalyptus branch, I was amazed at just how willing he was to go over, in loving detail, a complaint he'd already made several times. Now, again, I was astounded at not only how long and freely he talked, but the narrow slice of life he saw. Hasbrouck Diamond was definitely a horse in blinders. He was, as I had suspected, pierced to the marrow by Kris's betrayal. His hurt took up all the light the blinders allowed in; there was no room left to see that Kris had been focusing on issues of his own and that he, Diamond, his feud, his need for acceptance, his prospective film, were merely peripheral. As peripheral as was his own understanding that he had *murdered* Kris. For Hasbrouck Diamond the murder was merely an appendage to his hurt.

I spent the rest of the evening with Leila Sandoval, taking her statement (nothing new there) and listening to her bemoan the unfairness of life, an unfairness for which she, of course, had no responsibility. I left her in another cell awaiting transport to Santa Rosa.

Between those interviews, Vikram Patel called to tell me that the elder Mouskavachis and their four children would be arriving at the San Francisco airport the next afternoon. He had added, in a gleeful tone I hadn't previously heard from him, that his consulate, at the encouragement of the Nepalese government, would not be renewing their visas.

Sunday morning, which I had planned to spend in a whirlwind of apartment hunting, Howard and I devoted to alternately sleeping and otherwise taking advantage of the luxurious California King. I couldn't bring myself to wake up enough to admit this was my last day here.

When I did finally swing my legs over the side onto the plush gold carpet, it was two in the afternoon. Howard, who seemed remarkably tolerant of my pre-departure grief, brought me a cup of espresso. (He had become an expert at operating the machine. I had become a pro at letting him.) I could still have gotten dressed and looked at apartments. Instead I said, "I'm going to miss it here," and followed him for a last lovely soak in the tub.

The fog had lifted. The picture window across from the tub, of course, was clear, and below, San Francisco Bay was bespeckled with white sails. "Like dandruff on a blue-haired lady," Howard commented as he lowered his long tan body into the warm water. Clearly he had endured as much of my upscale melancholy as any decent Berkeleyan could stand.

I slithered down into the water, trailing my hand

along his arm. Then I leaned back against the edge of the tub and let the hot water lap halfway up my neck and thought again, I am going to miss this place.

I pictured Mr. Kepple's waiting porch, with its indoor-outdoor swamp and cacophony of botanical gizmos and irate neighbors. I was really going to miss this place.

On Howard, of course, the water reached only to his armpits. He reached one of those long arms over the edge and hoisted up a Carta Blanca beer. Taking a swallow he said, "Pereira and I had a bet on your murderer. I picked Bev Zagoya. Tell me how come I can be wrong."

"Do you mean that in the cosmic sense? Or just with this issue?" I reached for my espresso but it was too far away.

He handed me the cup, spraying water across my face in the process. I was going to miss seeing his lovely, wide, lightly muscled shoulders with the steam rising around them.

Keeping hold of his hand, I said, "Bev was right. Alive, Kris couldn't destroy her. But he could destroy this one expedition. Hasbrouck Diamond had everything committed to that. With Kris's announcement he'd have lost his place as honored supporter, his money, probably his house, and certainly what credibility he had in the film world. He'd have been left with nothing but gums."

Howard shifted his leg over next to mine. "Diamond'll get lots of them in 'Q.'" He laughed. "Bev Zagoya may not have killed Kris, but I wouldn't put money on that option having been far from her mind when she saw him wander into her lecture Thursday night. No wonder she ended it so fast."

Meandering down from his knees, droplets of steamy water outlined his thigh muscles. I rested a hand on his knee. "It's funny, Howard, if it hadn't been for the feud, Leila would never have brought Kris over here. And if not for the feud, she wouldn't have allowed him to stay with

Hasbrouck Diamond. And Diamond, Sandoval, and Zagoya might have realized that Kris was playing them all—except, of course, they were all too involved in playing each other to be able to compare notes."

Howard took another swallow of beer, put down the bottle, and sank lower into the water. It lapped around his neck. Another two inches of thigh emerged. "But, Jill, what about the killer eucalyptus? Did Diamond's nemesis, Sandoval, magically drop it on him?"

I sighed. "I want to go on record as being right about that branch. You cannot make them drop on cue. Even with the worst tree trimmer in Berkeley. Even with copper nails in the base and bacteria in the damp crotches. And in any case, it wasn't Leila who damaged the tree, not that she might not have, had she thought of it."

"Or Zagoya?"

"She was gone too much, in the Alps or wherever, to water anything regularly."

"Diamond, huh? Willing to lose his head, literally, to save his spot in the sun?"

"He was never in danger. The thing was, Howard, his chair was not right under the branch. If it had been, the branch would have fallen on him. Branches that size fall straight down. This one didn't hit him, because he wasn't sitting under it, he was just far enough to one side to escape with a scratch. At the time he hatched the plan for the branch to fall, he didn't care when it came down. He was just hoping that the implicit danger would be enough to force Leila to take out the trees."

"But *he* was liable."

"So he'd have had to pay to haul them out. He'd still have had his victory."

"Regained face, eh?"

"Right. It was he with his hose on the roof who kept the crotch wet enough to cause the branch to fall. And he got a rope around it in the dark of night and pulled to

181

weaken it. All he needed to do was check that Leila wasn't home. No one else would notice. He was the only one who could have done that."

"Then he sat back in the sun and waited? Every creak from the tree when the wind blew must have been a thrill. And they say the sedentary life isn't exciting." Howard laughed and shifted over so his arm was against mine.

Despite the heat of the tub a shiver ran through me. I realized I'd better talk fast. "That was his plan. But when he realized that Kris was going to destroy him, he hurried that plan along so we would be focusing on Leila by the time Kris died."

"Rather than himself."

"And his plans for Bev's expedition."

"It's nice that he's confessed."

I wriggled under his arm. "We would have got him anyway. Would you like to guess what kind of suntan lotion he used? Patchouli oil."

"Raksen will be unbearable."

"He wants to send a copy of the report to 'Police Beat.' He wants it headlined FOILED BY OIL."

Howard laughed, then pushed himself up and reached for one of the thick towels on the pegs nearby. "We could go upstairs and build a fire. With the fog it's cool enough."

Howard was going to miss The Palace, too, even though he would never admit that this was the Triple Crown of dwellings, as compared to his own Glue Factory Handicap.

I sat in the warm water watching the drops scurry down his back, over his firm butt, down his long sleek thighs. "I'm going to miss this place," I said. "I think I wasn't meant to rent an apartment; I was meant to housesit in palaces. To watch tall, sleek, red-headed men rise like Excalibur from the steamy depths of hot tubs. To live above my element."

Laughing, Howard reached over and pulled me up. Then his blue eyes narrowed into seriousness. "Jill," he began slowly, "I know you aren't wild about my house. You don't see the hidden beauty, the possibilities—"

"The fuses that blow whenever you use two appliances at once."

"Bedrooms that could be a study, a den, a music room, a hot tub/sauna even nicer than this."

"The guy who hosted the chanting group at four A.M.," I said, running a hand down his lightly tufted chest.

"The original mahogany once we strip the paint off the railings, and the mantel and the paneling in the dining room . . ."

"When you strip the bamboo that's grown up through the floor in the downstairs bathroom." I pulled his face toward me and gave him a kiss. "Howard, you are a superb man. You are wise, and clever, and discerning. But, dammit, you are the worst judge of houses in the entire city. You are the type of person who would have a beautiful new barn in your pasture and house your horses in a lean-to. You would see a knoll with a view of paradise and build that lean-to in the swamp at the bottom. You would—"

Howard was laughing. "I take it," he said through his laughter, "that this means you are taking me up on my exceedingly generous offer to give you a spot at the bottom of my lease and a room that adjoins my own."

A picture of my only real alternative flashed through my mind: Mr. Kepple's porch, with Mr. Kepple plugging in his hedge clipper outside. "Just for a while, Howard."

It was then that I saw the culmination of Berkeley syndrome, when the tomorrow you've staved off is today, when you come eye to eye with the pasture fence. Right then I saw that fence in a way that Leila Sandoval never would. It wasn't blank and gray and endless as I had feared. Close up it came into focus differently. Some parts of it could be okay.

Okay if the one tenant's beagle didn't howl all night every night and the former tenant's boa constrictor didn't slither up though the pipes.

But some parts of this arrangement were likely to be very nice indeed. I smiled at Howard.

But there was still one outstanding debt in this case to be settled. Tomorrow I'd deal with that. I would borrow Howard's Travelall and pick up the Mouskavachis from the airport (my own small remembrance for Kris). They would need someone to help them with the funeral, and finding a place to live, and getting inoculations for their children before they could be enrolled in school, and finding work, and lots lots more. It would be a big job for someone. Very probably a thankless job. But I knew how it could best be handled, best for the Mouskavachis and best for me. From the airport I would take the Mouskavachis to Telegraph Avenue, to Herman Ott's office. In private, Herman Ott would put up a squawk. But I knew Herman Ott, he'd end up taking the entire flock of Mouskavachis under his wing.